THE
SHEPHERD

STORIES OF CHRISTMAS

TOM CUNNINGHAM

Soft cover ISBN: 978-1-4866-2504-8
Hard cover ISBN: 978-1-4866-2506-2
eBook ISBN: 978-1-4866-2505-5

Word Alive Press
119 De Baets Street Winnipeg, MB R2J 3R9
www.wordalivepress.ca

WORD ALIVE
—P R E S S—

Cataloguing in Publication information can be obtained from Library and Archives Canada.

To Barb, my loving wife and partner in ministry.
Forty-one years and counting of sharing the wonder
and beauty of the birth of our Saviour.

Contents

Introduction

The Christmas story is one of the most compelling narratives ever recorded. Its beauty resides in its cast of characters: angels, mysterious sages from the east, shepherds, a working class family, a wicked king, and a baby.

But what really adds to the story's wonder and magnificence is its truth. It doesn't need any embellishment to attract us, and once attracted we discover a story that has the power to change lives.

The story has been told over and over again, to the point where there is some danger that familiarity can dull its edges and neutralize its power. It is too often treated as a cute baby story swaddled in layers of tradition, causing us to forget that Christmas is the celebration of God taking human form to live among us on the earth.

The other side of this coin is that many people, more and more all the time in our post-Christian era, have never heard the real Christmas story. They've heard the commercial version but haven't experienced the authentic rendering that has the capacity to effect positive change. The story's impact is more far-reaching than any other in the history of the world. Imagine God Almighty, sovereign God, sending His one and only Son to earth not to punish us for our sins but rescue us from these very sins so we might have eternal life.

Too often we whitewash the Christmas story and perceive only the soft glow of candles, seductive twinkling of lights, and alluring songs of the season. We forget about the cost of Christmas, and I don't mean the credit card bills that haunt us each January. We must remember the cost God bore on our behalf, giving up His only Son, and the cost His Son Jesus paid, giving up His place in heaven and being born as a baby in a stable and ultimately dying on a cross. This is all given willingly out of a love for us that's simply out of this world.

Christmas is upon us! To awaken us from sweet slumber and reignite in us the boundless joy and excitement the shepherds experienced that first Christmas Eve, and the hope this event has brought to countless people over the centuries, these stories attempt to peel back the layers of tradition, commercialism, and sentimentality. They aim to expose the pure beauty and love expressed by the coming of the Light of the world. This Light has the power to create life in our hearts, life of the highest level, life that not even death can extinguish.

These stories all had their beginnings as messages I wrote over the years, many of which were first delivered at Christmas Eve services. They are fictional, with a touch of the mystical. After all, the Son of God is the main character. And Christmas tells the story of one of the most amazing miracles the world has ever known.

Many of these stories are simple, and some may even think they were written for a child. Think of them as having being written for the child within all of us. They aren't long and don't contain complicated theological words. Isn't Christmas the story of a child? Did not Jesus Himself once say that we must receive the Kingdom of God as children?

And who knows? Maybe these stories will help someone hear the Christmas story for the very first time.

While there is at least one shepherd in several of these stories, they ultimately point toward the Good Shepherd, Jesus Christ. Here we see Jesus in all His majestic glory, His saving grace and eternal love.

We must never forget that the nativity story is but one chapter of the greatest story ever told. It's an incredibly important chapter, but one that shouldn't be read in isolation.

To that end, in numerous places the Easter account makes an appearance, since it is an integral part of the Christmas story. You can't have Christmas without Easter, and you can't have Easter without Christmas. Christmas is about the birth of the Christ child, whereas

Easter is about the death and resurrection of Jesus Christ, including the rebirth of all those who yield their lives to Jesus.

As you read these stories, don't be afraid to laugh or cry. But above all, don't be afraid to allow the Holy Spirit to bring this wonderful story to life in your heart. May the baby of Bethlehem, the Saviour of the world, be born in each of our hearts.

> O holy child of Bethlehem,
> Descend to us, we pray;
> Cast out our sin and enter in;
> Be born is us today.[1]

---

[1] Phillips Brooks, "O Little Town of Bethlehem," 1868.

The Shepherd

I could still hear the angry words just before the door slammed: "Get out, Roger, and don't bother coming back!" That had been three hours ago. I'd been homeless for three hours. The snow squeaked under my running shoes.

What a day. I'd gotten fired—well, that's what I called it. My boss had told me that my services were no longer required. I couldn't really blame him. I'd have fired me too. He had found a small amount of company product in my locker.

I knew how it had gotten there. For the past month or so, product had been going missing from the warehouse. Two weeks ago, a couple of guys at work had asked me to make sure a few extra boxes got on a certain truck each night as it left the warehouse. I hadn't cooperated.

Guess who was waiting to speak to the boss as I left with my pink slip, no doubt ready to ask for my job?

I went home and within an hour became embroiled in a verbal fight with my father. I knew he only tolerated me at the best of times, since I had refused to go to business school and join him at his accounting firm. To him, I was just a working class peasant with no ambition. He even called me a disgrace to the family name, told me that any lowlife could work in a warehouse; it took a "real man" to run a business.

He went ballistic when I told him that I no longer had a job—and he actually believed I had been stealing.

"How stupid could you be? You must have known you would eventually get caught."

I believe those were his exact words. And with that, I was officially removed from the family. Fired and disowned all in one day. And that day happened to be Christmas Eve.

Now what? Where would I turn now?

I tried a couple of hotels, but they were booked solid with travellers in for the holidays. And so I was left to wander the streets, still dressed in my work clothes.

After turning a few corners, I found myself standing at the bottom of the steps of St. James's, one of the biggest churches in the city. I'd never been in a church before. My father had always said that churches were for wimps. Only weak people went to church! Successful people went to the cottage or went skiing… the same things we did nearly every weekend.

The lights were on at St. James's and I heard the sound of singing coming from inside. I was cold, and in my father's eyes I was already weak and a loser. So why not go in?

I climbed the stone steps and opened the heavy oak door. The singing grew louder.

The ceiling of the cavernous foyer had to be twenty feet high, held up by beautiful stone columns. Giant chandeliers hung low, casting soft yellow light.

Directly in front of me was a door that opened into a very large room. Its ceiling was high and ornate. The windows had coloured pictures and chandeliers cast light down onto the hundreds of people sitting on fancy wooden benches. They faced the front, where an old man in flowing robes stood behind a lectern, upon which lay a large and heavy open book.

The man's voice was clear and strong. "And it came to pass in those days that a decree went out…"[2]

I wanted to go in. I supposed this was the church proper. It certainly looked like a church from the pictures I had seen.

---

[2] Luke 2:1, NKJV.

I was just about to enter when a man came up to me. "You can't go in there," he whispered. "There's a service going on. You must want the street centre. It's three doors down on the left."

"I just want to go in and see what's going on."

"You can't." He hesitated. "Well, I suppose you can, but you'll have to wait until the next appropriate time in the service."

Some of the people sitting near the back of the big room turned around to glare at me.

If this was church, I didn't want any part of it. I turned, headed back for the big wooden door, and reached for the latch.

The old man continued speaking behind me. "Now there were in the same country shepherds living out in the fields…"[3]

Even though I really wanted to hear the old man's story, I opened the door and felt the cold air on my face. Flakes of snow were starting to fall. Oh well. No one else in that church seemed to have wanted me to hear it. Besides, I had more important things on my mind, like figuring out where I would spend the night.

I started walking, not knowing where I was going. I just walked.

"Roger! Roger, wait up."

I turned to see who was calling my name but didn't see anyone I recognized. The only person nearby was an old man about twenty feet behind me. He was dressed in the most peculiar fashion, like one of those hippies I had read about from the sixties. He had a beard, long hair, and robes made of rough, well-worn material. In his left hand he held a walking stick taller than he was; it had a crook at the end, just like a cane. On his feet he wore sandals. No socks.

"Roger, wait up."

"Who are you? How do you know me?"

"Oh, that doesn't matter right now. Can I buy you a coffee?"

This was just too strange, but I was cold and lonely and the old codger appeared harmless. He was probably just a street person and I could have used the company.

"Sure," I replied. "But where will we go? It's Christmas Eve. Everywhere's closed."

---

[3] Luke 2:8, NKJV.

"No problem, my friend." He pointed. "Look."

Sure enough, across the street, amidst all the darkened storefronts, was a small coffee shop where the lights were still on. The open sign flashed its bright neon welcome.

We crossed the street and tried the door. Finding it unlocked, we entered and found a table against the back wall.

No one else was here except for a middle aged man sitting on a stool behind the cash register. He was reading a newspaper. When he saw us, he looked up and called, "What can I get you?"

"Two coffees," my companion called back. "One black, one... what do you take in your coffee?"

I shrugged. "Double cream, no sugar."

Soon there were two large hot cups of coffee on the counter in front of us.

"That'll be four-fifty."

The old man reached amongst all the folds of his robe and pulled out a leather pouch from which he produced two gold coins.

The server looked at the old man. "I can't take these. Did you steal them from a museum?"

My companion looked embarrassed. "No, I didn't steal them from a museum, whatever that is... I just forgot to exchange my money—"

"It's okay," I broke in. "I have a five. Here, keep the change."

The server smiled and wished us a merry Christmas.

When we finally seated ourselves at a table with a red gingham tablecloth, the old man spoke first. "So you got kicked out of the church, too? I did as well, just before you did. I thought I would go in and see what they did with the story, but I couldn't get through the door. The man you met, he called me crazy. Told me I wasn't dressed appropriately and to get lost. I'm sure glad God didn't say that to me the first time! He sure didn't tell me my clothes weren't proper for the occasion..."

"What do you mean, the first time? What occasion? What are you talking about?"

"It's like this, young man. Me and my shepherd buddies were working the hills around Bethlehem. There were some pretty big sheep farmers in the area and we were always in demand. The townsfolk couldn't get by without us, even though they didn't think much of shepherds. They said we were always dirty and smelled of sheep. So I've been kicked out of more than one establishment in my life, including the temple.

"Anyway, one winter night my buddies and I were sitting around a fire keeping warm and telling stories. The sheep were in the pen for the night, but we had to watch anyway in case any thieves or wild animals came by.

"Suddenly we saw this really bright light in the sky! At first I thought it was a shooting star, but it didn't go away, and out of this bright light—now stay with me, kid. This is going to sound impossible. As sure as fire burns, what I'm about to tell you happened. Out of this bright light, a being appeared and told us not to be afraid. This being told us that the Messiah, the Saviour of the world, had been born and we would find Him in a stable in town. He would be using a manger for a cradle."

I found myself remembering the words of the story being told in the church: *"Now there were in the same country shepherds living out in the fields…"*

"You're one of those shepherds, aren't you?" I said. "You were there. You were part of the story."

"Yeah, I was there all right. Seems like only yesterday. I can still hear the chorus of angels as they sang, 'Glory to God in the highest.' It still sends shivers up my spine."

"But what does all this have to do with Christmas?"

I thought the shepherd was going to fall off his chair. The look on his face would have caused milk to sour.

"What does all this have to do with Christmas?" he exclaimed. "What are you, an ostrich? Your head stuck in the sand? Young man, this story *is* Christmas."

"But that's not the Christmas I learned about."

"What? I can't believe this. What story of Christmas did you learn?"

"We learned about Santa Claus coming down the chimney and bringing presents. But only if you were good. We got some pretty great presents at Christmas!"

The old man seemed confused. "That's what you learned about Christmas? How common is this? How many others think this Santa Claus guy is the story of Christmas?"

"A lot, I guess. My friends all think so."

"Young man, I have something to show you. Come with me."

The table and gingham tablecloth vanished, along with the two partial cups of coffee, replaced by a field with a fire burning. Despite being night, the sky was filled with the most brilliant light. It blazed like the sun! And out of this amazing light came the most beautiful singing I had ever heard. All around us, shepherds fell to their knees and bowed in honour, fear etched on their faces.

The words from heaven were as clear as a bell: "Glory to God in the highest, and on earth peace to men on whom His favour rests!" This was followed by a choir that sounded like a thousand voices all praising God.

When the song finished, a single voice spoke out of the light, inviting the shepherds to go into town—Bethlehem, they called it—where they would find the Messiah, the Son of God, in a stable.

The brilliant light faded and the group of shepherds were left with nothing but the soft yellow glow of the fire.

My new shepherd friend spoke first, the fire casting shadows across his face. "I don't know about you, but I'm going into town to see what the angels told us about."

The others agreed, and soon we were off to town. They decided to try some of the inns, each one of which had a stable in which travellers could bed down their animals for the night.

The second inn we tried had a small stable out back, out of the way. We walked down a narrow passage until we glimpsed a light shining from the only window. The animals inside sounded very much awake.

When my shepherd friend tried the door, it opened and we entered. We saw animal stalls down the right side, but right in front of us burning lamps illuminated a woman sitting on a stool, gazing into a wooden feeding trough. A man stood behind her, also staring at the manger.

As we entered, the man and woman looked up.

Once the shepherds had explained what they had just heard and seen out in the field, the man motioned for them to approach. The sheepherders each took turns looking into the manger—and as they did, their faces filled with awe and their eyes became moist.

I was the last to approach this makeshift crib. I looked down and saw a baby, a beautiful baby boy. He looked like every other newborn I'd ever seen, except for one detail. His eyes seemed to be looking back at me with purpose, meaning, and love. Pure, perfect love. I felt my heart being filled with a kind of love I'd never known before. It wrapped itself around my heart as tears of joy streamed down my face.

Without knowing why, without even knowing who this baby was, I felt like I was in the presence of royalty. And not just any monarch! I knew this was a King greater than any other.

I wanted this moment to last forever. I closed my eyes, thinking that if I did so I could block out reality. Such was not the case. I opened my eyes and there before me was a table with two half-empty cups of coffee on it and the old shepherd sitting across from me.

"What was that?" I asked. "What just happened?"

"You just looked into the face of Jesus, the Son of God. You looked into the face of love. That's the Christmas story."

I still didn't understand. I didn't know what to make of what I had just experienced, except that I wanted more of it.

The shepherd spoke again. "Christmas is about the greatest and grandest expression of love the world has ever known. What you need to know, Roger, is that you are loved by your heavenly Father—"

"Wait! I have a Father in heaven?"

"Yes, you do, my friend. God has invited us to call Him Father and it's all because of what Jesus has done for us. You need to know that your heavenly Father loves you so much that He was willing to give up His own Son and send Him to earth to be our Saviour and restore us to His family as His sons and daughters. That's how much you are loved. Without Jesus, without His death on the cross—that's the Easter story—we are in a burning house with no hope of being rescued. But with Jesus? Well, He entered that burning house to save us. God gave His very own Son to save us from our sins, to rescue us from lives that are headed in the wrong direction."

That's a lot of love, thought Roger.

This overwhelming love enveloped his brain and flooded his heart. It was like a dam broke, allowing this amazing love to flow into every pore of his being.

"God loves me." As Roger spoke the words aloud for the very first time, they seemed strangely familiar and oh so comforting, like a warm cup of coffee heating one's body all the way down.

The old shepherd smiled.

I had received a lot of great gifts in my life. Every Christmas, my parents had made sure my sister and brother and I had the very latest toys and games. I had to confess that earlier in the evening part of my sadness had come from the fact that I wouldn't get to find out about all the great gifts they had planned for us this year. I thought I had overheard them saying something about a car…

But whoever this shepherd was, he had just given me the best gift I could ever receive, far more satisfying than any car. I felt love like I had never felt before.

I looked out the window of the coffee shop just as the sun started to rise. My sister and brother would be up now and half the parcels under the tree would be unwrapped. I wondered if they missed me.

"Tell me, my shepherd friend…"

But when I turned to face the old man, he was gone. All that remained was an empty coffee cup and a note:

Roger. Thanks for the coffee. I'll buy next time. Gotta go now.

That love you heard about tonight, don't let it slip through your fingers. Tell God you love Him. Give your heart to Him. He is your heavenly Father.

Go find a group of God's people, ones who will accept you for you. Let them share God's love with you.

One more thing: God will take care of you. In the Bible, there's a verse that says God will tend His flock like a shepherd. Can you believe that? He used us dirty, old, unpopular shepherds to describe how He cares for us.

Roger, always remember that you have a heavenly Father who loves you and cares for you like a shepherd cares for his sheep. And believe me when I tell you that no one is more committed to caring for sheep than a shepherd. God will never leave you.

Merry Christmas,

Your shepherd friend

God Became Man

Mark stopped just before entering his apartment building and looked behind him. There, rising above the rooftops, were the office towers downtown. The air was clear and crisp and the lights appeared to twinkle. The towers were at least five kilometres away, but their size made them feel close. Close yet so far.

He remembered the days when those towers had been his world. He'd been only one promotion away from a corner office and all the perks that went with it. He had earned a pretty nice six figure salary and he and his wife had owned a beautiful home on an acreage an hour north of the city, with two high-end cars and a cottage. There had been enough money left over every year for them to spend at least two weeks in the Caribbean.

But that seemed like a lifetime ago.

Mark would never forget the day when his boss had told him the company was downsizing and he was being let go. He would be granted a generous severance package and a letter of recommendation, but who was going to hire a fifty-one-year-old middle management executive?

Everything would have been okay—not great, but okay—had Maria not decided to leave him. She enjoyed the high life too much and it turned out that someone in the office had had his eye on her, and hers on him. As far as she was concerned, it had been a no-brainer. Lifestyle over love.

She'd taken a big chunk of Mark's settlement. According to the judge, she was entitled to it.

Mark took one last look at those office towers, then turned and opened the unlocked wooden door. A large piece of green paint fell at his feet. After climbing two flights of stairs, he came to his apartment door, the second on the right. Turning the key in its lock, he stepped into his home.

The expensive furniture of his past life looked out of place and didn't fit, but it was all he had. He couldn't afford anything different. As a matter of fact, money was scarce these days.

He placed the bag he had been carrying on the counter and began to put its contents away—a loaf of bread and frozen turkey dinner. That would be tomorrow's treat.

Turning on the television, he heard the announcer report that radar had just picked up an unidentified object streaking across the sky of northern Canada. Interceptor planes had been sent up to investigate. The object was a sleigh, driven by a man in a red suit and eight reindeer.

"Santa Claus…"

Mark startled himself for having spoken the name aloud. Santa had never brought him what he really wanted. All he'd ever wanted was for his father to stop drinking and yelling. And he had wanted his mother to stop crying. She'd tried very hard not to cry in front of him, but he had heard her nearly every night as he lay in bed, sobbing till his own heart ached.

Oh, she had tried hard to be a good mother. One year for Christmas, she had gotten him a new toque, blue and white with his favourite hockey team's logo on it. But on the first day back at school after the Christmas break, the school bully had grabbed the toque right off his head and stomped it into a slush puddle, staining it with salt and tearing it in several places. Mark knew there was no money for another.

Yelling, crying… crying, yelling… he couldn't escape these troubling sounds. Even as a grown man, he always cringed when he heard someone yelling.

After finishing school, however, Mark had caught a break. A man at his mother's church had heard that he performed well above average in math, and one day this man invited him and his mom to come to his home. The car in this man's driveway, Mark was sure, must be bigger than the tiny apartment he had grown up in!

It had turned out that the man wanted to give Mark an opportunity to earn a good education. Indeed, he offered to pay for Mark to attend university. He even recommended that Mark study business management.

And Mark did just that, ending up with a master's degree in business administration and a lucrative job. Then he had married Maria; in his eyes she had been like a goddess, recently descended from Mount Olympus. He had never seen a more beautiful woman, and she was smart and fun to be around. The same day he accepted the generous job offer, she accepted his proposal.

But that was three lifetimes ago. Some goddess. She had been more like the devil incarnate.

As he settled into his modest apartment, the anger and bitterness began rising to the surface of Mark's heart.

Look at all I did for my employer and all I gave Maria, he thought. *This is my reward? A crummy minimum wage job and this dump to live in alone?*

He shook his head in frustration.

Stop it, Mark, he told himself. *Don't let yourself go down that road again. You spent months on that road—and while you were there, you spent nearly all the settlement money and most of your savings. Don't go back. Look forward!*

At least he had a job. Not much of one, sure, but it *was* a job. And he had a roof over his head. He just had to smarten up and not let the past destroy him.

Mark had been having this fight with himself a lot less often lately, but it still reared its ugly head from time to time. He calmed down in front of the television, and before long he had dozed off.

When he awoke, a solitary figure on the screen was talking about God.

Oh great. It's Christmas Eve and I have to listen to religion...

He had no use for religion. As far as he was concerned, God was just a myth. Like Santa Claus. As a matter of fact, he had always thought it appropriate that Santa and God were celebrated at the same time each year.

He reached for the remote and tried to change the channels. Maybe he could find a late-night replay of a hockey game. But no matter what button or combination of buttons he pressed, this holy roller prophet man kept appearing. He was on every channel.

Even when Mark hit the power button, the TV stayed on!

As he tried to figure out how to silence this holy annoyance, he noticed that this was no typical TV preacher man. He wasn't scrubbed clean, without a hair out of place, shoes polished to military standards, wearing a suit without wrinkle. No, this man wore a plain blue shirt and jeans and he had a gentle expression on his face.

And his eyes were firmly fixed on Mark.

He stopped trying to silence this man and began to listen.

"Christmas is about Jesus voluntarily giving up his place in heaven, and all the glory and perks that go with living in heaven, to come to earth to be born as a baby in a stable with a manger as His crib. That's right, Jesus's first earthly home was a stable."

I can relate, Mark thought to himself. *I wonder what Jesus did wrong to get shafted like that. Was God just downsizing? Maybe He was trying to improve the bottom line in heaven. Maybe He had to get rid of a few middle management types, even at the expense of His own Son.*

The preacher continued, opening his Bible and reading. "In the beginning was the word and the word was with God and the word was God…"[4]

Mark chuckled to himself sarcastically. Well, that explained it all pretty clearly.

"The word is another word for Jesus," explained the preacher, "Jesus was with God since before creation. In fact, Jesus is part of God. He is God Himself."

That surprised Mark. So Jesus wasn't just another expendable middle management person? He was God Himself. How did that work?

Before he could try to figure out this puzzle on his own, the preacher went on. "Later in the same passage, the Bible says, 'And the word

---

[4] John 1:1, NIV.

became flesh and dwelt among us.'⁵ Another translation says, 'And Jesus moved into the neighbourhood...'"⁶

When Mark heard those words, a strange tingle went up his spine—not a chill, but a warm shiver. This preacher man was no longer a one dimensional talking picture on a TV screen; somehow his presence was right there in his apartment.

More importantly, Jesus no longer seemed like a myth. In a way, He seemed somehow very real and present, something Mark couldn't explain.

He felt overwhelmed and confused as he kept listening. The baby had been born in a stable but was no less than God's own Son. This birth had been no accident. Jesus hadn't come here against His will.

But why? Mark wondered. *Why would anyone, including God, choose to give up so much?*

It just didn't make sense, according to Mark's world. No one ever gave up anything voluntarily. You fought for everything you could get. You held on to everything you could, at any cost.

Mark had heard the Christmas story before. Every year his mother had played what she called "real Christmas music," songs that told of Jesus being born in a manager, with shepherds and wise men with expensive gifts. He had even gone with his mother to a Christmas Eve service once.

But none of that stuff had stuck. No, it was just a fairy tale. God hadn't been able to make any of the yelling and crying stop, so why believe in Him?

Mark's only tip of the hat to Christmas was that once a year around this time he would write out a few nice-sized cheques and send them off to charities. Then he waited for the tax receipts.

Come to think of it, he didn't even really know what these charities supported. He just got their requests in the mail and they looked legitimate so off went the cheques.

If this preacher was to be believed, God had done more than send a cheque. He'd sent His very own Son to get involved in a personal way with the people of the world. He had moved into the neighbourhood!

---

⁵ John 1:14, NKJV.
⁶ John 1:14, MSG.

This thought somehow touched Mark's heart. A strange but pleasant feeling began to fill him, something he'd never felt before. Was this what love felt like?

While Mark pondered this question, the speaker on the TV said something he wasn't prepared for and left him scratching his head: "He came to that which was his own, but his own did not receive him."[7]

What did that mean?

Mark thought he understood. Jesus had made this great big sacrifice for the people He had considered to be His own, the people on His team, but they had rejected Him anyway. What a bunch of ingrates, not to appreciate what Jesus had done for them.

"And do you want to know who these people were who didn't receive Him?" the preacher asked. "They were, and still are, the ones who don't make time for Jesus. The ones who think they don't need Him in their lives. The ones who think Jesus is only a myth. The ones who do good deeds by giving money to charity but don't make room in their hearts for Jesus."

"Enough is enough," Mark spoke aloud to the TV screen. This guy was getting a little too personal. It was Christmas Eve, no time to get all serious and heavy duty.

But as uncomfortable as Mark felt, for some reason he needed to hear more. He wanted to know what came next in the story. He was realizing the real reason Jesus had come to the earth—for people like himself. Christmas seemed to be about God taking a personal interest in regular people.

For nearly the very first time in his life, Mark began to feel in his heart what it meant to be truly loved. His mother had loved him, true, but there had been too much going on in his family for that love to be fully expressed. He had known he could trust her, that she would protect him, but they hadn't talked much. She had never seemed to be available.

And what of his own marriage? Mark had to be honest. He hadn't really married for love; he had married for looks. Maria had been the best looking girl at school and all the guys had wanted her. Mark had gotten her, making him feel like he'd won the lottery.

---

[7] John 1:11, NIV.

Some win that had been! Now she had taken off with half his money. The closest he had come to feeling true love was the feeling he had for his two children. He had tried to show his love for them by giving them everything they wanted, but that hadn't always worked. If he didn't give them exactly what they wanted, they let him know it. Then Mark felt as though he had let them down, as though he didn't love them enough. And where were they now? With their mother?

They aren't here, that's for sure, he thought.

But now Mark felt love in his heart, love as he had never experienced it before. God had taken a personal interest in his life because He loved Mark.

The pastor was reading from the Bible again. "This is love: not that we loved God, but that He loved us and sent His Son as an atoning sacrifice for our sins."[8]

Mark found himself in territory he had never visited before. He hadn't experienced love so pure, unconditional, and sacrificial. There were always strings attached in his world: "you scratch my back and I'll scratch yours." That was the motto he had always lived by. Success meant doing favours to get favours. No one ever just did something nice because they *loved* you! No, there was always an ulterior motive.

But this wasn't the case with God. He came with pure, unmerited love. He had stepped out of heaven and into the body of a human being—a baby, no less, born in a stable.

"The word became flesh and dwelt among us…"

Until this night, he had always measured his value and worth by his job, his bank account, his house, his cars, and his holiday plans. His standing in life had been tied to his accomplishments and accumulations. So when he'd lost his job and his wife, he had lost everything. He'd felt totally worthless.

What about this new feeling of love? He seemed to have value exactly as he was, if this preacher was to be believed.

He certainly didn't have value in the world's eyes. He hadn't heard from any of his former coworkers. There hadn't been any calls or offers for help, and he understood why. He had treated others the same way.

---

[8] 1 John 4:11, NIV.

He hadn't had any time for lowly people. What happened to them was too bad, but he still had work to do. The corporate world taught that others were only as valuable as what they could do for you.

That isn't how God thinks, he realized.

Mark could barely grasp the concept that God had loved him even before he'd loved God, back when he'd been a self-centred bigshot. Even then, God loved him enough to give him His only Son.

Giving and loving were connected, he now learned. Giving was about more than writing cheques or dropping off donations at the food bank. It involved giving of oneself, getting personally involved with others. It was about giving not out of duty, responsibility, or self-gain but out of a motivation to love as God first loved us.

For the first time, Mark felt peace in his heart. He felt as though he were being wrapped in a blanket of unconditional love, a love intended just for him—Mark the convenience store clerk, the former executive with a multinational corporation; Mark who had never made time for God or gone to church or read the Bible or prayed; Mark who had been so full of himself and obsessed with worldly gain that he hadn't needed God.

The new Mark understood that God loved him, and in return he was beginning to love God.

He looked out the window of his humble apartment and noticed a flashing neon red sign across the street: *The Inn.* It was a street mission. Mark had only ever walked swiftly past it until today.

Now its sign provided the only colour in his room at this late hour, as his life was transformed from monochromatic black-and-white to vivid colours. He hadn't discovered this life while occupying his eighteenth-floor office, or while spending time with his beauty queen wife, or while relaxing on a Caribbean beach.

I found it once all that was gone, he thought. *Once I was all alone on Christmas Eve in a small apartment above the drycleaners with a TV dinner waiting in the freezer.*

On the TV, the speaker preacher began to pray… and then the screen faded to black without Mark even touching the remote.

He stood up and walked to the window, looking over the sign of the street mission towards the gleaming office towers in the distance. He no longer wished to be part of that life; he saw those steel and glass walls more as a prison than a palace.

Suddenly, he noticed that the anger he had been carrying around in his heart was gone. He felt like a prisoner who had been released from jail.

Mark fell to his knees, tears streaming down his cheeks, and knew that Jesus had visited him.

"Jesus, thank You for coming to me tonight," Mark prayed. "You still leave heaven, don't you? You still come to Your people, even the ones who don't know they're Your people. Thank You for making Yourself known to me. Thank You for coming into my neighbourhood. Thank You for loving me unconditionally, for filling my heart with Your love. Thank You for rescuing me from myself and my anger. I'm sorry that I didn't make room for You in my life. I don't want to be like those people who rejected You. Jesus, I give You my heart. You are the best Christmas gift ever..." He trailed off, but then remembered one more thing. "And God, help me to love You and others the way You love me. Amen."

* * *

One year later, Mark stood on the street outside The Inn and looked up at the building which housed his apartment, the same one where his life had changed on that fateful Christmas Eve.

He had found new purpose as a bookkeeper, cook, and worker for the street mission.

He still lived in that same apartment, but it was no longer a reminder of what he didn't have; rather, it recalled the rich blessings that had been lavished on him by his heavenly Father.

He wanted to live among the people he served and who kept bringing such unexpected gifts of faith and love into his life.

Abandoned

If the first clunk had sounded bad, the second one sounded fatal. The engine light came on and Jacob's SUV slowly lost power. By the time he had manoeuvred it to the shoulder of the highway, there was no sound coming from under the hood.

Oh great, he thought. *So a $100,000 SUV sounds the same as a $30,000 one when it breaks down. Now what?*

It was 3:00 p.m. on Christmas Eve and he was still two hundred kilometres from home.

The Christmas part wasn't all that important to Jacob. He had never really cared much for the holiday. As for family, they wouldn't be home and his wife had been alone on Christmas before. She would manage.

His main concern was that he had invited the head of a large supply company to attend a Christmas eve dinner with her husband, and it was scheduled for 7:00 p.m. Only four hours away. He had timed his trip to be home just in time to shower and be ready for dinner at seven.

Now that wasn't going to happen.

His wife could hold her own at any dinner party, but Jacob knew the value of the missed networking opportunity. He would have had the chance to firm up a multimillion dollar contract with his guests, the Andersons.

The Andersons loved Christmas, he knew, and this was the first year none of their children would be coming home to celebrate with them. They would be lonely, which is why he'd invited them for Christmas

Eve. The only stipulation was that they would have to come over after their church service at 5:00.

Jacob knew he could fake a traditional, sentimental Christmas, at least for one night, if it meant solidifying a good business connection. But that was all down the drain now.

His first call was for a tow truck, which was thirty minutes away. Next he called his wife, to inform her she would be on her own with the Andersons. He thought he heard a sigh as he hung up.

Twenty-five minutes later, the tow truck showed up. The news was not good.

"Well, sir, the closest repair centre is a hundred kilometres away," said the tow truck operator. "By the time we get there, they'll be closed until the twenty-seventh. Is there someone who could come out from the city and pick you up?"

"No, not tonight. Maybe tomorrow."

While Christmas was no big thing for Jacob, he did have a shred of decency. He wouldn't ask one of his employees to give up part of their own Christmas celebration to help out the boss.

"Is there a hotel around here where I could stay for the night?" Jacob asked. "I'll make arrangements to get home tomorrow."

"No hotels in these parts, but I do have a place for you to stay. My aunt runs a bed-and-breakfast just up the road in a little village called Bethlehem. It's quiet right now. Does most of its business in the summer. I'm sure you could stay there."

Jacob nodded. "Great. Why don't you call ahead and make arrangements with your aunt? Then you can haul this priceless piece of junk to that repair centre."

Just like that, Jacob had a place to stay.

Half an hour later, he was being dropped off in front of an old two-storey Victorian redbrick home on the main street of Bethlehem. He was greeted at the door by his host and hostess for the evening, Peter and Shirley Shepherd. He felt at home almost immediately.

The second floor room was more than ample with a queen bed, a sitting area with big bay window, and its own private bathroom.

"Dinner will be at five," Shirley informed him. "We're eating early tonight so we can go to the Christmas Eve service at seven."

With that, she disappeared downstairs to put the finishing touches on dinner.

Just before five, Jacob appeared in the dining room. Peter was there, as was a young boy of about six years old.

"This is our grandson, Andrew," said Peter, proudly introducing the lad. "He lives up the street but wanted to eat dinner with his grandma and grandpa tonight."

"Pleased to meet you Mr. Jacob." Andrew held out his hand and Jacob shook it.

After dinner, Jacob headed back to his room. He wasn't going to let a quiet evening go to waste, so he pulled some papers from his briefcase and began crunching numbers. Sales had been down in the east and he wanted to see why.

Just as he settled in, he heard a knock on his door. He opened it to find young Andrew standing in the hall.

"Hi, Mr. Jacob. Will you come to church with me tonight? I'm Gabriel in the play. I know my lines! 'Glory to God in the highest and on earth peace to men on whom His favour rests.'[9] So will you come? Please!"

"No, but thanks for the invitation."

Andrew's face fell—and when he turned to walk away, Jacob closed the door. No one, not even a six-year-old, was going to get him to go to church. Not on Christmas Eve. Not ever.

A few minutes later, he heard the front door close and the house was quiet.

Five, then ten, fifteen, and twenty minutes of pure uninterrupted silence ensued. He was really getting into the east coast numbers when suddenly he was startled by a very loud banging on the front door. He didn't know if he should answer the door or call 911.

He opted for the former. After all, what could go wrong in a little town like Bethlehem?

---

[9] Luke 2:14, NIV.

He made his way downstairs and slowly opened the door. There appeared to be nobody there. No one on the walkway or the street. Not even the sound of a car.

He was just about to close the door when he looked down. That's when he saw an old car seat and a beat-up carryon bag. He bent down and was shocked to discover an old moth-eaten blanket... and in the blanket, a baby. A living, breathing baby.

The child's eyes opened and there was a big yawn.

Instinctively, he picked up the car seat, baby and all, and took it into the front hall. He then went back for the bag.

A baby? Jacob hadn't touched a baby in years. He'd hired a nanny for his own kids. He just wasn't all that into babies—or children, for that matter.

But here he was, all alone with a baby.

He pulled the blanket back and found a note.

Please, whoever finds my little boy, please take care of him for me and give him lots of love. I can't care for him. I have no money and nowhere to live.

The baby started to cry and Jacob looked around as if someone might materialize out of thin air to help. But no one came.

The hard truth now dawned on him. He was going to have to take care of this baby until the Shepherds arrived home from church.

He tried to lift the baby up, and he did so awkwardly. At first he didn't support the head properly and the baby's head fell right back. The crying grew louder. Jacob laid the child right back down, worried that the head was going to come right off at the shoulders!

Taking a deep breath, he tried again. With a supportive hand placed behind the head, he gently lifted the child and cradled the boy in his arms. At last the crying stopped. When the infant looked up into Jacob's face, he thought he could see a smile.

The smile faded.

"Ooooh, what is that smell? No, it can't be. Tell me it isn't so." He broke out in a cold sweat, speaking to no one in particular. "No you don't. You aren't getting me to change you…"

As if right on cue, the baby began crying again.

"Besides, I don't have any diapers." He looked around. "Wait a minute, I bet I know what's in that bag…"

Sure enough, he dug inside the carry on bag to discover two diapers and a host of other baby-changing paraphernalia.

It was no easy task, but a half-hour later he had a clean and dry baby, even if Jacob himself looked a bit green.

I'll just wait until the Shepherds return from church, he consoled himself. *They'll know what to do.*

And they did. Shirley took charge of the baby and Peter called the police, who stopped by to take our statements and ask whether Shirley and Peter could keep the baby until the proper authorities could respond. The officer also thanked Jacob for caring for the child. He had no doubt saved the baby's life.

Once the police left, Jacob excused himself and headed off to his room, thankful that the ordeal was over. For him, the past couple of hours had been more stressful than getting a letter from the Canada Revenue Agency about an audit. He would just get back to his reports.

Try as hard as he might, though, he couldn't get that baby boy out of his mind. When it became evident that he wasn't going to get any work accomplished, he decided to go to bed and get a good night's sleep so he could settle everything in the morning and return to the city.

The bed was warm and comfortable, but sleep didn't come. His mind was full of questions. What kind of parent would abandon their child on the front porch of a stranger's house on a cold winter night? What if he hadn't been there? Would that baby have frozen to death? What an uncaring, incompetent parent! If they had been one of his employees, he would have fired them right on the spot.

Then it hit him that he had done something similar to his own children. No, he hadn't left them on the front porch for a stranger to raise, but he hadn't been there for them. Tonight was the very first time he had changed a diaper in his entire life. He certainly hadn't gone to dance recitals or soccer games.

Yes, he had abandoned his children and let nannies and neighbours raise them, following the same model his parents had used on him and his sister.

Feeling angry and lost, tears welled up in his eyes. He had never felt this way before. He tried to stifle the emotion by getting up and walking around the room.

He tried to shake it off. This was silly.

As he walked by the door, his bare foot stepped on a piece of paper that hadn't been there earlier. He must have dropped a page from one of his reports.

He bent over, picked up the paper, and turned on the lamp. It wasn't a page from a report. It was the Christmas Eve program from church. Someone had slipped it under his door and attached a note.

My name is on page 3.
—Andrew
P.S. Missed you at the service.

On the cover was the picture of a mother and father and a baby. They were in a stable and the baby lay in a manger. Jacob had to think for a moment to place it. He'd seen the story a long time ago, part of a made-for-TV movie. It was the baby Jesus and his parents, Mary and… Joseph…

Underneath the picture were some words, written in fancy script:

This is how God showed his love among us: He sent his one and only Son into the world that we might live through him. This is love: not that we loved God, but that he loved us and sent his Son as an atoning sacrifice for our sins.[10]

Jacob read the words a second time. They didn't make sense to him, but somehow he knew they were important. They contained a message

---

[10] 1 John 4:9–10, NIV.

he needed to hear. An inner desire had been awakened in him, and that desire needed to be satisfied.

And it was all started by a baby.

"This is how God showed his love among us." Jacob couldn't get those words out of his head. Love hadn't been a big part of Jacob's life. Business, success, money, appearances… that's what really counted. He didn't even love his wife. She looked good on his arm at appropriate functions and she was a wonderful hostess at dinner parties. But he treated her more like a business asset than a wife.

He found himself dwelling on that word, *love*, and not just any kind. This was God's love, a love so deep that He had been willing to part with His own Son and send Him to the world—as a baby, no less. A baby that was born in a stable. And what had the world given in return?

Jacob's memory travelled back to a snowy night when he was only twelve, watching a movie on TV about Jesus. He became very troubled, recalling that the world had crucified that man.

Nice, he thought. *Real nice. So much for love.*

His looked back down at the program and the verse written on it: *"This is love: not that we loved God, but that he loved us and sent his Son as an atoning sacrifice for our sins."* So Jesus's death on the cross had been a sacrifice, made on humanity's behalf.

He sat heavily in the big easy chair in the corner, feeling like he was in over his head. Until now, he'd just thought of Christianity as a big hoax, a money grab. He hadn't given any time to it. But now it was starting to make some kind of sense—and that scared him. He was a man who calculated everything to make sure he always stayed in control. But this was taking him out of his comfort zone… and he was no longer in control.

Jacob had always been able to compartmentalize his life, locking away the painful parts and keeping them at a safe distance. He could always justify a questionable business practice by saying it was for the good of the company. But now?

His thoughts were taking him in a direction he didn't want to go. He couldn't stop them.

Jacob closed his eyes and imagined himself being abandoned on the front steps of a house. Left alone. He had often felt that way as a youngster, unloved by his parents. He had few happy childhood memories, only loneliness and sadness. His mom and dad had always been busy with business and friends. He had suppressed these unpleasant feelings as best he could, and it got easier to leave his feelings behind when he got out into the business world. He just had to keep making money and working harder and harder. Money wouldn't abandon him like his parents had. And money could get him whatever he wanted.

But the money *had* abandoned him. No sooner had he made it than the emptiness and hunger had returned to his heart. If he was honest with himself, he had known for some time that money and success really weren't the answer. They would never take away his feelings of abandonment.

He remembered something that had happened to him when he was six or seven years old. It was Christmas Eve and he'd cried himself to sleep because his parents had chosen to go away and leave he and his sister with the nanny.

Had he been abandoned, though? No. He was realizing that someone had cared for him—even loved him, if he dared himself to go there. Just as he had rescued that baby earlier, God had rescued him, so to speak, by sending His Son Jesus to earth.

Jacob's mind snapped to attention as he recalled the verse from the program again: *"This is how God showed his love among us: He sent his one and only Son into the world that we might live through him."* His one and only Son.

"I must be important to God for Him to give me His only Son," he murmured. "That's quite a sacrifice."

Earlier that evening, when he'd discovered the baby, for a moment he had felt annoyed at the inconvenience. The baby had ruined his evening.

That's nothing compared to how much it cost God to show His love to me, Jacob thought. *I could have been an inconvenience to God, but instead He treated me with love.*

But why would God love him? Jacob realized that he'd abandoned his share of people over the years, including his own family. Including God. He was far from perfect. His business practices hadn't always been aboveboard, and he'd been unfaithful to his wife.

God still loved him.

"This is love: not that we loved God, but that he loved us and sent his Son as an atoning sacrifice for our sins."

He couldn't be sure exactly what that meant, but somehow it seemed to imply that God's love and Jesus's sacrifice had caused his sins to be forgiven. For him to be given a fresh start. He just had to make room in his life for Jesus—a lot of room. He couldn't ignore Him or abandon Him any longer.

As the clock struck 2:00 a.m., Jacob realized he hadn't slept a wink. He got up out of the easy chair and climbed into bed with a deep sense of peace, a serenity unlike anything he had ever experienced.

Just before he dropped off to sleep, the last thought he had was about the police officer who had thanked him for being there for the baby and saving its life.

But Jacob now knew that the baby had really saved his life.

The Sacrificial Lamb

Nelson felt angry and bitter. He even had pure hatred in his heart. In fact, he hated everything about life.

Two months ago on a Monday, he went to work on top of the world. Before leaving for home the previous Friday afternoon, he had received an email not from his local manager but from a manager at the head office in Vancouver. The corporation was going to make a very important announcement on Monday at noon, one that involved Nelson in a very big way. Over the past few weeks, there had been some pretty solid hints coming his way that he was in line for a significant promotion. That had to be what was coming on Monday.

And sure enough, the company sent out a press release on Monday at noon that named Nelson to his new position.

Then, on Tuesday, Nelson discovered that his first assignment would be to carry out a very controversial decision the company had made—a decision that was going to generate a lot of opposition. While he didn't like the thought of having to defend it, Nelson felt he could handle the damage control. In a week or two, it would all blow over.

That's not how it played out. The general public was far more upset than Nelson had anticipated. And when they demanded blood, it was Nelson's blood that was shed.

Five days into his new position, he was terminated. He took the fall for the company's decision.

As he reflected over what had happened, Nelson realized he'd been set up. The plan all along had been to promote a middle management type to be the sacrificial lamb. He was expendable. The company could maintain their controversial stance while firing Nelson to prove that they were listening. The severance package was a small price to pay for them. Everyone won… except Nelson.

Actually, the severance package was too poor a consolation compared to the humiliation of having been used and abused. And now he was unemployed. The circumstances exerted a huge strain on his home life, too. He was consumed by anger, bitterness, and that darkest of all feelings—hatred. Even his faith in Almighty God, once the rock he had built his life on, was gone. God had let him down.

Christmas was only a couple of weeks away. This had always been the best time of the year for Nelson, like an oasis in a desert. He didn't mind confessing that the warm and fuzzies of the season had often been a welcome relief in a life otherwise overstuffed with, anxiety, and the feeling that life was simply passing him by. Hardly a day elapsed that he didn't bring home some work from the office. His phone would ring at 9:00 p.m. or later with someone pleading for help.

But none of this at Christmas. This was the season of peace and rest.

There would be no such relief this year, though. Nelson's heart was too full of the poison of resentment and rancour, the toxic anger that coloured every thought and seasoned every word he spoke. He was a prisoner and nothing about Christmas would bring him release.

Nelson was sitting in his den, languishing in anger and self-pity, when he heard a phone ring in another room. It was his wife's cell. He heard her carry on a conversation, though he couldn't make out exactly what she was saying. That didn't matter. As long as he didn't have to talk to anyone! He had been refusing to answer his own phone, and his wife knew that if anyone tried to get him through her, she was to say he was unavailable.

Suddenly, Peggy entered the den. "It's our pastor from church. He wants to speak with you."

"I'm not available."

"But he insists. He says it's very important."

Nelson was silent for a good two minutes.

"Well, are you going to talk to him?" Peggy asked with a note of pleading in her voice.

"Here, give me the phone." His anger surged as he took the phone from his wife. "I'll speak to him all right, but only to tell him I have no use for his religion or for his God."

Peggy walked out as Nelson brought the phone up to his ear.

"Pastor, just so we're clear, you won't be seeing me in church anymore," he announced. "I have no use for you or for your God. He's ruined my life."

Nelson's finger hovered over the end call button, but a force stronger that him blocked him from pushing. It was like an invisible finger was preventing him from cutting off the pastor.

"Nelson, I know you're angry. I get that." The pastor sounded genuine. "But I have something very important to share with you, something I think you need to hear. Can you come to the church this afternoon? Say, around 2:00 pm?"

Nelson was ready to deliver a very emphatic no, but instead he heard himself say, "Okay, but I'll only give you a half-hour."

Before the pastor could respond, Nelson found the courage to press the end call button.

He felt confused after he put down the phone. Bewildered would have been a more accurate word. First the invisible finger had stopped him from ending the call too early. And then his voice had been hijacked!

For the rest of the morning, Nelson stewed about his impending visit with the pastor. And at church, no less. On God's turf. He should have insisted that the pastor come to the house. Then he could have told him to leave.

At lunch, Peggy knew to keep her distance. The couple hardly spoke a word to each other.

"I'm going to see the pastor this afternoon," Nelson said when they were cleaning up. And that was it.

Peggy just nodded, with the slightest of smiles tugging at the corner of her lips.

Almost an hour later, Nelson was sitting in his car, parked in the church lot at five minutes to two. Should he go in or just leave? One, two, three, four minutes passed. Nothing the pastor could say or do would change his mind. He was done with God.

As his phone alarm sounded, reminding him of his two o'clock appointment, Nelson opened the car door. He made his way into the church and headed towards the pastor's office. He would at least give the pastor a piece of his mind. That might be cathartic.

The church was quiet as he passed through it. At least no one else would hear his rant.

"Come on in, Nelson," the pastor said through the open door to his office.

His voice was too cheery for Nelson's liking. This wasn't a social call. Nelson planned on speaking his tough words and then leaving. No conversation required.

"Can I get you anything? Maybe a coffee?"

"No thanks," Nelson said, surprising himself. He hadn't used the T-word in over two months. There was nothing for which to be thankful.

"Have a seat, my friend." The pastor gestured to the comfortable sofa. Nelson sat, but much against his better judgment. "Nelson, I want to start by saying that my heart is broken for you. Peggy told me the whole story. I can't even imagine the pain, even anger, you must be feeling. You were betrayed in the most insidious way. I haven't stopped praying for you since I heard the news. And I don't blame you for not coming to church. I want to assure that I didn't invite you here to talk you into coming back to the services. That's something you and God will have to work out when you get back on speaking terms."

These words caught Nelson off-guard. It wasn't what he had been expecting at all. He'd thought it would be all about putting things behind him and getting on with his walk with God. It would be about being a good Christian, even if that meant getting thrown under the bus. About putting on that fake smile and trucking on for the Lord, regardless of how he felt inside.

Instead the pastor's words disarmed Nelson.

"So you must be wondering why you're here," the pastor continued. "Well, it's not to ask how you're feeling. I know how you feel, because I would likely feel the same way if it were me. I'm always here for you and willing to chat, when and if you wish. I've already told you that. When you wouldn't take my calls, I texted you. The reason I asked you here is to offer you a job."

More words Nelson hadn't been expecting. They dropped on him like a bomb. A job? No way. He would never work at the church, never work for God. Not now, not ever.

The pastor went on before Nelson could respond. "Perhaps you are aware, my friend, that I'm on the board of Missions International. We have missionaries in over sixty countries, including Canada and the U.S., spreading the good news about Jesus Christ. While we try to keep our costs down to ensure that most of our resources go to support our fieldwork, we do have several full-time administrative positions. We have a chief financial officer, a bookkeeper, a senior administrator, and a CEO. Our CEO is retiring and we've been praying about a replacement. When the board met the other night, your name came to my mind, and it wasn't by way of a gentle reminder. Your name appeared in front of me in neon lights. I closed my eyes and there it was. I thought, 'What a great idea!' You have the business experience needed for this position, but you're also a man of God. Now, we can't come close to matching the pay you're used to, but you could more than live off this salary. So what do you say, Nelson?"

Nelson didn't know what to say. This hadn't been on his radar at all. He had known he would need a new job at some point, of course, since the severance package would run out eventually. But working for God? He wanted to reject the offer and walk out, never looking back.

But he couldn't. He couldn't figure out how to say no. He couldn't even find the strength to get up from the sofa.

"You know, there are some similarities between the situation you find yourself in and the situation Jesus found Himself in during His time on earth," the pastor remarked. "Think about it, my friend."

The pastor had no right calling him "my friend." Nelson was fuming mad. He was no friend of anyone who was a friend of God. But no words came out.

"It's Christmas," the pastor continued, oblivious to the smouldering wick of anger that threatened to erupt into full flame. "The time we celebrate Jesus leaving His home in heaven and coming to earth. Now, we usually think of all the good stuff that goes with the Christmas story. There's the birth of the baby and all the warm and fuzzy feelings and traditions we've created around this story. But there's also a painful, sacrificial side to Christmas we must never forget. Our heavenly Father gave up His one and only Son and sent Him to earth knowing all the nasty things that would happen to Him, including death on a cross."

Nelson began to fidget. He knew where this was going and didn't like it one little bit.

"I'm not saying your situation and Jesus's are the same. They are as different as night and day. Jesus knew what He was doing. He knew the whole plan for salvation even before He came to earth and accepted His Father's will voluntarily. You were manipulated and deceived. You had no idea what the company was planning. But this one thing you have in common: you both know what it's like to be a sacrificial lamb, taking the fall for another's misdeeds. You were tricked into being the fall guy. Your sacrifice was nefarious. Jesus's sacrifice was to defeat sin. Now, Nelson, you have the opportunity to work for the sacrificial lamb, to continue His work in saving those who are lost in the darkness of sin."

The room went silent for a full five minutes. That's when Nelson got up—and as he got to the door, he turned.

"I'll let you know my decision by this time next week."

The pastor smiled as he heard Nelson drive out of the parking lot. What he hadn't heard was Nelson's prayer as he sat in his car before leaving: "Lord, I'm so mad at You, yet here You are offering me a job working for You. What gives?"

And in his heart, Nelson heard a still small voice. *"Consider it my Christmas gift to you."*

Nelson smiled for the first time in two months.

Zechariah

The house literally stood in the shadow of the temple. Every afternoon, just before sundown, the house of the Lord cast a shadow over the home of Zechariah and Elizabeth, if only for a few minutes.

Zechariah, a priest at the temple, and his wife loved the Lord. When the shadow enveloped their home, they felt the Almighty wrapping them in His arms.

But events were about to unfold that would take this couple's relationship with the Lord to a whole new level.

"Zechariah, if you get chosen to burn the incense in the Holiest of Holies, please promise me that you'll remember to pray that we'll have a child," Elizabeth called to her husband. "I know you have other prayers to offer up to Almighty God, but please remember."

"Oh Elizabeth, when will you give up this dream? I know how hard it's been for you. For me, too, but especially for you. I know how the other women shun you and speak unkindly about you. I've heard the whispers. I've seen the hurt in your eyes. I don't know why God hasn't blessed us with a child, but that's just as it is. We're not bad people. In fact, I couldn't have chosen a more upright woman to be my wife. We follow the Torah and keep all its commandments. We love the Lord with all our hearts."

"Please pray, Zechariah."

"But you're nearly seventy… and I'm nearly eighty. There's no human way we could ever have a child. Please, dear, we have to realize it just isn't going to happen."

"What about Sarah and Abraham? They were nearly a hundred years old when they had Isaac."

"That was a couple of thousand years ago, back in the age of miracles when God was more active among His people. It's been over four hundred years since we heard any message from God. He promised us the Messiah… and then nothing. We must not expect things to change now. We'll only get our hopes up and be disappointed."

I hated to talk to Elizabeth this way. She was such a wonderful wife. I didn't want to pour cold water on her dreams, but she had to be realistic. We were old. If her womb had been barren when we were young, it would only be more so now.

The division of priests I belonged to was beginning its period of service in the temple, so I would be living there for the next two weeks. There were several dozen priests in my division so I had very little chance of being chosen to burn incense in the Holiest of Holies. We were chosen by lot and my name had never been called.

Even if I was called, I would have to pray for specific things. For peace and the welfare of our people. For the Messiah to come. It would be too presumptuous of me to add a selfish prayer. Besides, Elizabeth and I had prayed for a child for years, and none ever came.

A look of disappointment, and even hurt, crossed over her face.

"Okay," I said, relenting. "Sometime during the next two weeks I'll pray for God to bless us with a child."

A little smile came to Elizabeth's lips and a glimmer of hope showed in her eyes.

"Now I need to finish getting ready," I added. "Are my robes clean?"

"Yes, they're laid out on the bed and your good sandals are with them."

I went off to finish getting ready.

After dressing, I met Elizabeth at the door. She looked me right in the eyes. "Don't forget to say that prayer. I'll be praying it right here along with you." Her voice was strong and full of anticipation. She never gave up.

I reassured her, gave her a kiss, told her I loved her, and set off for the temple.

As I walked along the road, excitement began to build. These two weeks would be holy, and I always wondered at the back of my mind whether I would be chosen to enter the Holiest of Holies, the most sacred chamber in the temple.

I knew deep down that I would never be chosen. The odds were against me, but I could still dream. I guessed something of Elizabeth's optimism was rubbing off on me.

I also had a question for God. Why were good people, like Elizabeth and myself, chosen to suffer through childlessness? The common assumption was that the barren womb signalled the presence of sin. But in our case, it wasn't so. We were righteous. We weren't perfect, but we hadn't stepped out on God in any big way.

Bad things still happened to good people. Suffering wasn't always a sign of sin. I had learned this much from experience.

Upon arriving at the temple, I put my questions on hold and joined the other priests as we got on with our responsibilities.

The first few days went as expected, but on the fourth day we gathered early in the morning—even before breakfast, as was common practice—to choose the priests who would burn incense in the Holiest of Holies. The priest in charge had a container of straws, two of which were shorter than the others. Those who chose the short straws would have the privilege of burning the incense.

The second priest to draw was chosen. Since my turn wouldn't come until the end, I knew my chances were low. The second short straw would be long gone by that time.

I watched as priest after priest chose their straws. Long, long, long, long, and so on… long, long… My choice was coming in three, two, one… long, long, long…

I put my hand into the container, took hold of a straw, and pulled it out.

I couldn't believe my eyes. It was short! I maintained my composure outside, but inside I was busting. I wanted to shout at the top of my lungs. What an incredible honour! What a privilege! Before this day was out, I would have the honour of going into the most holy place of the temple.

I had to practice. We had all been trained for this moment. We knew the liturgy inside and out, but I needed to rehearse it. I didn't want to make a mistake. I had to be perfect.

My role would be to light the incense during the afternoon liturgy when the temple was filled with worshipers, all waiting for me to come out and pronounce the blessing of God on them. I wondered if Elizabeth would be there today.

I spent the rest of the day going over the prayers and words I would say. Then I went over them again, and yet one more time.

At just the right moment, I entered the preparation room where the special robe was placed upon me. I was so nervous. Butterflies attacked every part of my stomach.

I picked up the container of incense and was escorted by the other priests, just as I had done many times, to the entrance to the Holiest of Holies. There they stopped and left me alone as I stepped into this most sacred of places.

The room was quiet and dimly lit. A fire burned on the altar and I smelled the smoke. Goosebumps rose on my arms. It was so holy a place, I could scarcely breathe.

I approached the altar. The fragrance was so sweet.

I was just about to begin the prayers when the whole room filled with the most incredible, most brilliant light. I closed my eyes, wondering whether this was a dream, but when I opened them again the light was surrounding me.

In the midst of the light, a being appeared, dressed in robes so white that they dazzled, even hurt my eyes. It became clear to me that this was an angel. I had never seen an angel before, but I knew this must be one.

My heart stopped. I was frozen with fear. The appearance of an angel could only mean bad news. What had I done? This was my one opportunity to burn incense, and somehow I had ruined it. I must have done something wrong. It had to be my fault. Was there a sin I hadn't confessed?

I felt sick to my stomach, certain I was about to hear a word of judgment against me.

When the angel spoke, his voice was smooth and soft and pure. "Do not be afraid, Zechariah; your prayer has been heard. Your wife Elizabeth will bear you a son, and you are to call him John. He will be a joy and delight to you, and many will rejoice because of his birth, for he will be great in the sight of the Lord. He is never to take wine or other fermented drink, and he will be filled with the Holy Spirit even before he is born. He will bring back many of the people of Israel to the Lord their God. And he will go on before the Lord, in the spirit and power of Elijah, to turn the hearts of the parents to their children and the disobedient to the wisdom of the righteous—to make ready a people prepared for the Lord."[11]

My mind could hardly take this all in. A baby? Elizabeth was going to have a baby! We were going to have a son.

No. Surely this was all a joke, a figment of my imagination. I wanted this to happen so I'd created this great dream. I probably wasn't even here in the Holiest of Holies. I would wake up at any moment…

I looked at the angel. "How can this be? How can I be sure of this? I am an old man and my wife is an old woman. We can't have a baby."

"I am Gabriel," the angel replied. "I stand in the presence of God, and I have been sent to speak to you and to tell you this good news. And now you will be silent and not able to speak until the day this happens, because you did not believe my words, which will come true at their appointed time."[12]

I opened my mouth to reply, but nothing came out. While I processed this new development, the angel disappeared and the bright light went with him. The Holiest of Holies was lit once more by the fire that burned on the altar and a few candles.

For several minutes, I was completely paralyzed. I couldn't move. I tried to speak again and again, but nothing came out. I couldn't

---

[11] Luke 1:13–17, NIV.
[12] Luke 1:19–20, NIV.

concentrate on the prayers I was supposed to offer up; I even forgot some of them.

How would I go out and pronounce the blessing on the people? No doubt they were anxious for my return. I had been much longer than usual... but maybe if I went out my voice would return...

I made sure the incense was left burning and made my way out to the people. I stood before them and I heard them murmuring. They knew I had been gone too long.

When I opened my mouth to explain, no words came out. Silence reigned. I tried to use gestures, acting out what had happened, and some seemed to understand that I must have seen some kind of vision.

Back in my room, other priests came by wanting to know what had happened. I couldn't tell them. I really just wanted to be left alone.

Once the door closed and the last priest left, I collapsed onto my bed. Over and over, I replayed the events of the evening. A messenger of God had appeared to me. This hadn't happened to anyone in more than four hundred years. God had been silent, choosing not to speak to His people since the last prophet.

And now it appeared that He had a message for His people, or at least he had one for me and Elizabeth. We were going to have a baby, a son, even in our old age.

What was it the angel had said? "Your prayer has been answered..." My prayer for a child had been answered! I hadn't even been able to pray in the Holiest of Holies, let alone for a baby, and it had been a very long time since I had prayed that prayer. I'd given up, though I hadn't told Elizabeth. It had seemed useless, a waste of breath. No way could we have a baby.

I guess no one should ever underestimate God. He had taken His time but come through for us.

That's God, isn't it? I thought to myself. *I must always remember that things run best when they run on God's schedule, according to His timing. I guess I give up too easily sometimes. Patience. That's what I need. I need to learn to turn every circumstance in my life over to God, who knows what's best for us. He knows what suits our lives better than we do.*

Back in religious class, we learned to wait on the Lord and never get ahead of Him. That's when things could go wrong.

God really does hear our prayers and answer them—maybe not on our time, or even as we wish, but He does hear and answer. And it's always the best answer. When we try to force God to do things our way, or stop expecting Him to act, life pulls us down. We get angry with God and our faith suffers.

I went to sleep that night with all these thoughts churning through my mind and my heart. Even though I had been a priest all my life, I realized that I needed to grow my faith. I needed to trust God and expect Him to act in unexpected ways and even do the impossible.

* * *

The next morning, I excused myself from my regular duties and went off on my own. I needed more time to think. There was so much to process that I was overwhelmed.

I was a righteous man. A good man, a priest, a servant of God. I followed all the rules. But being good wasn't enough. Being good had to be partnered with faith. And being good and being faithful weren't always the same thing. We could be near perfect in goodness, at least as far as the law was concerned, and not have faith.

And now, because of my lack of faith, I couldn't speak. The angel had told me that because of my unbelief I would remain silent until my child was born.

I need more faith God. Increase my faith, Lord. And while You're at it, tell me why—why did You wait so long to answer our prayer? Explain Your timing.

While I was asking this question, I happened to look down. On the ground between my feet was a beetle that had somehow got turned over onto its back. Its feet flailed in all directions as it tried to right itself.

I watched it for a few minutes as it struggled with no success. At that point, I reached down and gently turned it over. Away it scampered. Without a word of thanks, I might add.

Then it hit me: Elizabeth and I were in an impossible position in terms of have a child. We were too old. It just couldn't, wouldn't, happen from a human point of view.

But God sometimes waits until we're completely helpless before He intervenes, I reminded myself. *To be mean? No. To show that He is God and can do things we can't.*

He can do the impossible, all while taking the credit. That way, we could see that no matter what obstacles the world puts up to stymie our faith, God wins every time. No power on this earth, or above or under it, could be equal to or greater than the power of almighty God. All things are possible with Him. If only we learned that, we could do so much more.

We would be so much better off if we would stop putting God in a box, limiting Him and His work to our own abilities and limitations.

Elizabeth had been right when she'd told me not to give up. I had to keep on praying for a child.

That afternoon, I resumed my regular duties and carried on for the rest of our two-week term in the temple.

When I finally returned home, Elizabeth had heard all about my vision, but not about its content of course. By writing notes, I told her about the angel's message to us. As Elizabeth read the story, the glow on her face became more and more brilliant, until she beamed like the newly risen sun.

"I knew it, I knew it! We're going to have a baby, a son, and he will prepare the way for the Lord." Elizabeth was bursting with excitement. "The Messiah's coming and our boy will be a part of that incredible moment. Oh Zechariah, God is so good. So good!"

We hugged and cried tears of joy. Our burden had been lifted.

A few weeks later, Elizabeth became pregnant. Nine months later, our son John was born. As we named him, my voice came back.

I was so full of joy and thanksgiving to God. He does still do miracles. God is all-powerful, even sovereign over the barren womb. It didn't bother me that I probably wouldn't live to see my son grow up. All that mattered was that I had a son. And because of the fulfilled promise,

I also knew the Messiah was coming. Maybe not in my lifetime, but soon.

"The Messiah is coming…"

I must have said this aloud, for I heard Elizabeth call from the next room: "Did you say something?"

"Yes. I said the Messiah's coming soon."

But how many would recognize Him when He came? I lost myself in thought once more. How many would believe and welcome Him? I could have missed out on the blessing of fathering our little boy all because of doubt and my stubborn unbelief.

If people want to experience and know the Messiah, they will have to believe it is He. And what of those who come after and never have opportunity to see Him with their own eyes? They'll need to believe in Messiah in their hearts. And just as surely as this little fellow is right here in front of me, the Messiah will come and be born in the hearts of all who will invite Him in.

The Baby

I should never have allowed my wife to talk me into it. I had known this would happen. In just a few hours, I would have to lead the Christmas Eve service—and nothing was ready. The house was in chaos. There was no quiet place to work and I had just found out there hadn't been time to do laundry and I had no clean dress shirts. Only hours from conducting the most important and best attended service of the year and no clean shirt.

But what did that matter? I hadn't had the time to perfect the service the way I liked anyway. It was all a disaster.

It had been a crazy idea from the beginning, inviting the Taylors to stay with us until they got back on their feet.

Three weeks ago, my wife came to me and asked what I thought of the idea. Jack Taylor had been laid off three months earlier and found no steady work. They had run out of rent money and were about to be evicted.

"So why not, Andrew?" she pleaded with me. "We've got the room. It will only be until Jack gets a job. Then they can get an apartment of their own."

"But it's not just Jack. It's his three kids, and one's a teenager. And Marcia is expecting number four any time."

"That's all the more reason to let them stay with us."

My protests fell on deaf ears and I reluctantly agreed to let the Taylors stay, but only until Jack got a job.

This had led to three weeks of chaos, and now this disaster. I was doomed.

"Andrew, call 911!" my wife suddenly yelled from another room at the top of her lungs. "Marcia is ready to have her baby!"

Oh great, I thought as I fumbled for the phone. *This is just what I need, a baby on Christmas Eve. Talk about the wrong time for a baby to be born. I have a service to do and I'm not ready! I certainly won't look ready either. A baby... umph.*

Suddenly the room began to spin and I felt weak. I sat down on the sofa as everything went black. I tried to open my eyes, but they were already open; it almost seemed like I was moving, but my legs were still.

The dark slowly lifted and I couldn't believe what I saw. I was no longer in my living room but on a movie set of an old town, except without any cameras or lights or a director. I couldn't see anything modern.

The streets were crowded with people, old people and young people and children all dressed like they had just stepped out of a Bible picture book. There were no cars or asphalt or concrete sidewalks, only donkeys and camels and the scent. It smelled earthy. No, worse; it was like barnyard at midday on a hot summer day. I could also detect the tang of strong, spicy food. Merchants were selling fruits and vegetables from roadside tables. And above the noise of hundreds of people walking and talking, there was the squawk of chickens.

Over to my left were a group of musicians playing instruments I had never seen before, singing songs I couldn't understand. No one had their heads down looking intently at smartphones, trying to read texts and walk at the same time.

In fact, there was no sign of any technology at all. All I could see was dust and dirt in every direction.

Up on the right, a group of men listened as one of their number appeared to tell a story. I was going to eavesdrop to see if I could figure out where I was and what was going on, but then I realized I didn't know the language. It was all gibberish to me.

But as I walked by, I began to understand what they were saying, as though I had a translator in my head.

The storyteller was an old man who pointed to an old building across the street.

"My friends," he said, "I used to own that place."

Sure enough, the building had a faded sign with letters I couldn't begin to decipher. As the afternoon sun shone on those worn-out letters, I read the word "inn." Even my eyes were translating now.

"Made a nice living at it too," the old man continued. "Sure had a lot of interesting guests over the years. I had some of the best rooms in town, so we attracted all the visiting dignitaries. Members of the Jewish Council often stayed with us. But let me tell you about the most notable guest I ever had, although I didn't even know it at the time…"

His voice trailed off and he looked away. The group of listeners waited for one, then two, then three minutes. Not a muscle twitched, not an eye blinked.

"It was one of those hated taxation periods when our beloved Romans decided a census should be taken," he finally said. "This meant everyone had to travel to their birth town. Bethlehem sure was hopping. I had every room filled for three straight months. I might not like the Romans, but they sure helped the bottom line on more than one occasion."

I lifted an eyebrow. *Bethlehem… so that's where I am. Really? How did I get here?*

It didn't seem possible. I must have fallen asleep and dreamt all this.

"Anyway," continued the old man, "this one night—it was getting pretty late, well after the evening meal—a young couple showed up. The husband came in and wanted a room for the night. I looked out the door and there was his very pregnant wife, sitting on a donkey. The husband spoke with a northern accent. I guessed he came from Nazareth, and he was dressed the part. His clothes were rough and plain. I could see they'd both travelled a long way. They were dirty and tired. Very tired.

"'I need a room,' the man pleaded. 'It's nearly time for the baby to be born.'

"My heart went out to them, but what could I do? I had no rooms left and surely there weren't any rooms available for miles around.

"'No relatives to stay with?' I asked.

"'They're all gone now, but I'm in David's family tree. I have to register here. It's the law.'

"As this man spoke, I had an idea. There was a stable out back where the travellers kept their donkeys and other animals. It wasn't great, but with a blanket or two the straw would make a good bed."

"'I'm really sorry to pester you, sir, but I really need a bed for my wife,' the man said. 'Please, anything at all. I'll pay whatever you want, even if it's in your stable.'

"'Actually, that's just what I was going to suggest. I'll get some blankets. No charge.'

"'Really? Thank you, kind sir, thank you.'

"And the husband went out the door to bring the good news to his wife. An hour later, the young couple was safe and comfortable and asleep on a bed of straw.

"The evening just got busier and busier, and every few minutes someone else came to the door pleading for a room. Some left dejected, accepting the circumstances, while others got angry. They swore and cursed and went on for a few minutes. One even knocked over a lamp and nearly burned the place down. I could tell I wouldn't be getting much sleep that night.

"Just after midnight, I looked out and noticed several of the town's shepherds walking down the lane that led to the stable. It was a bit peculiar to see them in town at this time of night, but I was busy and couldn't leave my desk to see what they were up to. Besides, it wasn't totally unusual to see shepherds down near the stable. After all, animals are their business, right?

"A little while later, I heard the loudest whooping and hollering I'd ever heard. I looked out and saw those shepherds running out to the street acting like crazy men, making the wildest racket. I ran out and told them to be quiet. I had enough trouble turning people away! I didn't need the guests I did have getting upset. Obviously these men had been drinking.

"Well, when I confronted them the shepherds assured me they hadn't had a drop of wine.

"'So why the hollering?' I asked.

"'Because we saw Him, just like the angel said. The Messiah was born tonight.'

"Their story made no sense at all. Angels? The Messiah. There was no way. It had to be the result of the shepherds drinking. They had seen the pregnant couple back there and invented the whole story.

"Just then, more people arrived at the inn and I had to take care of things. I got so busy that I didn't bother to check what was going on back in the stable. I should have! Besides, I figured the Messiah wouldn't be born to a couple form Nazareth with a stable as his birthplace. He was destined to sit on the throne of David. Certainly he would have much more refined parents, not to mention the best care and probably a palace for a home. Those crazy shepherds... they were just a bunch of party animals and troublemakers who didn't know what they were talking about.

"The next morning, I finally got a chance to check on the couple. But they were gone. Apparently the shepherds had known of a place with a proper bed and cradle for the baby. That's right, I said baby. I found out many years later that the shepherds hadn't been the problem that night. I was. And because of it I missed the opportunity of a lifetime. I should have made time for that couple and followed up on what the shepherds told me. But I had more important things to attend to..."

The old man grew quiet again. His eyes looked saddened at the opportunity he had missed.

"But I've met Him now. I've met the most important guest who ever stayed at my inn."

The sadness lifted from his face and was replaced by a warm and happy smile. The creases around his eyes loosened and revealed the man's joy.

"The other day, I was in the holy city and heard a man talking by the side of the street, much like I'm doing now. Afterward I discovered his name was Peter. For some reason I'll never know, I felt compelled to stop and listen. I usually just go into the city, do what I came to do, and get out as fast as I can. I certainly don't take time to listen to strangers talking about things I know nothing about.

"But this time was different. It was like I couldn't walk away. My feet seemed to be stuck to the ground. And I'm glad they were. The more Peter talked, the faster my heart raced. He was telling about a man named Jesus. My ears perked up when he said this Jesus fellow was born in a stable in Bethlehem over thirty years ago. Jesus grew up and became quite a speaker. Then came the miracles and finally He declared Himself the Messiah, sent by God to save us.

"Well, I thought, if that was the case He didn't do a very good job. The Romans are still in charge! But Peter wasn't finished. He told about how Jesus was betrayed by His own people and arrested. They hated Him that much, and it only got worse. They were able to talk the Roman governor into sentencing Jesus to death by crucifixion. What a story! But even that couldn't compare to what I heard next. This Jesus fellow? Well, He didn't stay dead. Three days after dying, He rose from the grave. Today He's in heaven as our Saviour.

"Apparently we have it all wrong about the Messiah. He came not to save us from the Romans, but from our sins. That's why He died on the cross. He died in our place, for our sins, and when He rose from the grave He defeated even death itself, all so we could be forgiven and have eternal life.

"After Peter finished explaining all this, I approached him and told him the story of the baby who was born in my stable. Peter took me back to a house where he was staying. The other followers of Jesus were there as well and Peter encouraged me to tell them my story, and they in turn told me more about Jesus. That's when I understood that the baby born in my stable that night long ago was the Messiah. The shepherds were right, after all.

"At last, one of the men asked if I wanted to meet Jesus. Of course I did! But it was too late, since from what they told me He had gone back up to heaven. 'Yes, that's true,' I was told. 'But you can still meet Him, and He can live in your heart. Thirty years ago, you made room for Jesus to be born in your stable. Now you need to make room in your heart so He can be born in your heart.' He explained that I could make room by not being too busy for him, as I had been on the night of His birth. All I had to do was tell Jesus I was sorry for the times I hadn't made time for Him, and confess any sins I had committed and invite Him to be king of my heart. I did this and felt Jesus come alive in my heart. I've finally met Him personally!"

At that point, the talk became gibberish again. I saw the old man's mouth move, but I could no longer understand a word he spoke. But that was okay. I had more than enough to think about. Somehow, and I don't know how, I had just heard the Christmas story as told by the innkeeper himself. The very innkeeper who had been so busy that he missed the birth of Jesus.

Suddenly, I felt very sad. Very empty. It had been a long time since I'd thought about Jesus in a personal way. At one time, years ago, Jesus had been very real to me. I had met Him personally and invited Him into my heart just like the innkeeper had finally been able to do. As a matter of fact, I'd had a very close walk with God.

But then I got busy. Busy with family, yes, but also busy doing God's work… so busy that I forgot to keep up my personal relationship with Him. I let my church work take over my life and take me from God. I hadn't made any room for God on a personal level. My only connection with Him was professional.

Then it hit me. Had I not just said that Christmas Eve was the wrong time for a baby to be born? I'd forgotten what Christmas was all about. I had gotten so concerned about a clean shirt, an inconvenient birth, and preparing a service that I couldn't celebrate the birth of Jesus.

In fact, Christmas is the perfect time for a baby to be born!

"Andrew, call 911," my wife said. "The baby is coming and there's no time to get to the hospital."

I looked around and found that I was back at home in my living room. I made the call and within minutes the paramedics had arrived.

That night at the Christmas Eve service, dressed in a wrinkled shirt, I spoke about how we all get so busy in our lives that we forget God and lose touch with Him personally. It's even easy to forget what's really important to God. We only think about what we think is important to Him. We don't make room for Jesus in our hearts.

I continued my Christmas Eve message. "Jesus Himself had so many demands on His time, yet He always made time for His heavenly Father. When things were busiest, or when He was most tired, that's often when

He went off to find a quiet place to pray. I have to confess that I haven't prayed like that for years. My prayers sounded more like what you say in a business meeting than a conversation with God. The words of the Psalm writer come to mind: 'Be still, and know that I am God.'"[13]

* * *

After the service, I came home to a quiet house. The Taylors were at the hospital, and so was my wife. She had phoned the church, though, to assure me that mother and baby were well. It was a boy.

"Be still, and know that I am God." I repeated those words aloud. And as I did, I felt a waterfall of peace and calm flow over me and fill my heart with a feeling I hadn't experienced for years. A desire and passion for God took possession of me. I just wanted to get down on my knees and talk to Him. I had so much I wanted to say and I wanted to hear what God had to say to me.

As I knelt down, a vivid thought flashed through my mind: *God is no longer just my boss. He's my heavenly Father.*

"God, I'm sorry for treating you like my business partner instead of my heavenly Father," I prayed. "In place of making room for You in my heart, I only made room for church work. I really want to reconnect and get back into a close walk with You. I want You to be reborn in my heart tonight. I want to love You and know Your love for me, not just work for You."

As I continued to pray in a way I hadn't prayed for a very long time, I didn't hear the door open and my wife enter the room.

"The Taylors wish you a merry Christmas," she said, "and their new son Andrew is doing just fine…"

---

[13] Psalm 46:10, NIV.

The Unwanted Gift

Robert raced down the stairs and around the corner, running into the living room a full thirty seconds ahead of his younger brother and sister. It was Christmas morning and there were gifts to open, toys to play with, and no time to waste.

He heard a voice from upstairs. "Don't you kids open any presents until your mother and I get down there! We'll be there in two minutes."

The three children, who only moments earlier had picked out their first gifts to open and had already gotten ready to pull the trigger on the wrapping paper, now fell silent. They knew they would be in trouble if they opened even one gift too early. Something about Mother and pictures and wanting to catch all the excitement on her tablet... and Dad always said that half the fun for him on Christmas Day was watching the kids open their presents...

The three very anxious children sat on the sofa, so quiet they could hear the second hand on the clock in the hall. One minute, two minutes, three minutes, three and a half minutes...

They heard footsteps on the stairs and knew their parents were coming.

Robert couldn't hold back. "Come on, you guys, hurry up! It's Christmas and there's some serious present opening to do here."

"We're coming, we're coming," said Mother. "Be patient."

With that, Mother and Father rounded the corner. Mother was already aiming her tablet where she thought all the action would be.

"Okay, kids, away you go."

And with that, the children bounded off the sofa and hit the floor directly in front of their presents. The two youngest children just grabbed and tore. Paper and bows and ribbon flew in every direction, new toys appearing every minute or so.

Robert, being older and more mature, or so he liked to think, took a more methodical approach. He wanted to savour the moment. He had been planning for this very day for nearly a year.

Just after Christmas last year, he had first seen *it*. And when he saw *it*, he wanted *it*. He told his parents about *it*, but they responded with the number one response learned in parent school: "We'll have to see."

All spring and summer, Robert went down to the store to look. He even mentioned it at home from time to time, but the response was always the same.

"We'll have to see..."

Then Robert had the idea to ask for it for Christmas. His parents wouldn't be able to say no. So he made it very clear that this was the present he most wanted for Christmas.

Now the moment had arrived. The wait had been so long, but it would soon be over. Very soon.

The time had come.

Robert surveyed each of his gifts carefully. First he sized them up and then picked each one up to test its weight.

There. This was it. This was surely what he had been waiting for. The right size, the right weight.

He set that present aside. Once he opened it, nothing else would matter.

In a very methodical manner, Robert lined up his presents with the most sought-after one last. Carefully he removed bows and ribbon. He was too mature to tear the paper like his little sister and brother.

As he opened each present, he grew more excited. They were pretty neat, except for the one from Aunt Janet; she always gave the children pyjamas. Who wanted pjs for Christmas? He was going to have to have a talk with Aunt Janet someday.

When all the presents were opened and only one remained, Robert approached it reverently. He carefully removed the bow and checked the gift tag: "To Robert. Love, Mom and Dad." Robert was so excited that his hands began to shake.

He removed the tape at one end of the gift, and then the other. But before he removed the paper, he couldn't help himself; he took a peek inside the end of the present.

He stopped cold. A look of stunned disbelief combined with extreme disappointment covered his face. First one eye and then the other teared up, but he was too mature to cry, at least in public, so he quickly dried his eyes and simply put the half-opened gift back under the tree. All eyes were on him.

His little brother spoke first. "What's wrong, Robert?"

Before Robert could say anything, his mother looked at Robert's little brother and said, "Shh, just leave Robert alone for now."

Robert's mother or father didn't say a word about the gift and Robert didn't say anything to them. He wasn't sure why he kept quiet. Maybe it was the shock and disappointment. Maybe he was just too mature to complain.

The day wasn't a total loss. Robert did enjoy some of the other gifts he had received, but when he went to bed that night the half-opened present remained under the tree.

And there it stayed all through the next day and the next. And the next. In fact, it stayed there until after New Year's.

Two days after New Year's, Robert went out playing during the afternoon. When he came back inside, the tree was down and the half-opened present was nowhere to be seen.

As the year progressed, Robert thought less often about the present that wasn't. The following Christmas, he got what he asked for. For the next few years, in fact, his gifts matched his wishes.

The years passed. First came high school graduation, then university graduation, followed by marriage and his own children. He didn't often think about that half-opened present anymore. He had stored that memory away in the archive of his mind and only revisited it once in a while, usually when he was triggered by other disappointments in life.

One year, his wife surprised him. It was December 24 and just before he left for work she said, "Robert, let's you and I and the kids go to a Christmas Eve service tonight."

Robert hadn't been to a Christmas Eve service for years. When he was little, he had gone to church and Sunday school every week. And every Christmas, he and his brother and sister had been in the Christmas pageant at church. He even got to be Joseph one year.

But that was a long time ago. His parents had gotten busy on Sundays and there had been hockey and swimming and well. Other things just slowly took over until they didn't even go to the special services anymore.

"You want to go to a Christmas Eve service tonight?" Robert asked, not sure if he had understood her right.

"You used to go to church," his wife replied. "Come on, let's go. We don't have to be serious about God or anything crazy. But the candles and the carols… it kind of gives me goosebumps just thinking about it."

"Well, there isn't any hockey or dance or anything else tonight. So why not? I guess it wouldn't hurt."

"Great! I'll get the kids together."

"Hey. I don't have to wear a tie, do I?"

"No, but it would be nice if you got a little dressed up."

When they finally arrived, the church was crowded. There was hardly a seat left except right up front. But that was okay. It was Christmas Eve and the candles did look beautiful. And the music? Well, it was divine. Robert hadn't heard music like this since the last time he'd been in church on Christmas Eve over thirty years ago.

The service began and Robert actually enjoyed it. The carols were all familiar and it felt so good to hear the Christmas story again. "In those days Caesar Augustus issued a decree that a census should be taken of the entire Roman world…"[14] Robert was really getting into this service.

Then the pastor began a short talk by asking a question. After looking out over everyone seated in front of him, he asked, "Do you ever wonder how God feels on Christmas Eve?"

Robert felt as though the man was talking directly to him.

---

[14] Luke 2:1, NIV.

"For us, Christmas is probably the most exciting time of the year," the pastor continued. "It's a time of real joy and celebration. There are parties and presents, lights and laughter. But what about God? Christmas Eve marks the moment He gave up His Son, the moment He left home to come and live on earth. And what's even harder is that God knew exactly how we earthlings would treat His Son. What a wonderful gift He gave us! Yet from the get-go, His gift was ignored and rejected and even unwanted."

Robert squirmed, starting to remember that Christmas long ago...

"Let me draw your attention to a verse in the Bible. *He came to that which was his own, but his own did not receive him.*[15] What a tragic verse! Jesus came to His very own people, but they did not receive Him. Jesus was the long awaited Messiah. For centuries, the Jewish people had been waiting, watching, and wanting the Messiah to come. Their hearts ached as they waited. But when He sent the Messiah, for the most part people rejected Him. He wasn't what they thought He would be. He wasn't what they expected. He wasn't what they wanted."

Robert's heart burned as he flashed back to that present under the tree. The long wait was over, but then he peeked through the wrapping paper of the present and saw that it wasn't what he expected...

The pastor's voice brought Robert back to the present. "Almost from the beginning of Jesus's life, He was rejected in one way or another, just like an unwanted gift. First there was King Herod. Jesus was barely two years old when He and his parents had to flee Bethlehem. Herod had heard that a king was born a couple of years prior and became very jealous. He started killing all boys two years of age and younger.

"Later, it seemed there was always someone against Him, trying to take Him down. The religious and spiritual leaders of His day didn't like Him. He was becoming popular and His ideas clashed with theirs. They wanted Him dead... and they got their wish. Three years after Jesus began His ministry, He was executed on a cross. Even His close friends and followers rejected Him. One of His own disciples turned Him in to the authorities and had Him arrested. Another denied even knowing Him. If ever there was an unwanted gift, it was Jesus.

---

[15] John 1:11, NIV.

"But dear friends, God didn't allow all this rejection of His Son to cause Him to just throw His hands up in the air and give up. Three days after Jesus's death, God raised His own Son to life. He brought Him out of the grave. The grave and death and sin were defeated once and for all time. God did that so those who did receive the gift of His Son, even those today, could have eternal life in all its wonder and power.

"Do you know what the next verse says? Remember, John 1:11 tells us that Jesus came to His own, but His own did not receive Him. But then we read, *'Yet to all who did receive him, to those who believed in his name, he gave the right to become children of God.'*[16] It's not too late to reach out and accept the unwanted gift. Receive it and become a child of God."

Robert could feel his eyes moistening, but he quickly rubbed them dry. He was too mature to tear up in public.

The service concluded with a prayer and rousing rendition of "Joy to the World." Afterward Robert asked his wife to drive home.

That night, Robert tossed and turned. In the morning, when the kids announced they were headed for the tree and all the presents, he called out, "Don't touch a thing until your mother and I get there. You know how much she enjoys taking your picture opening the gifts."

That afternoon, Robert and his wife and kids piled into the SUV and set off on the two-hour drive to his own parents' house. Robert knew exactly what he had to do when he got there.

At first it was bedlam. Organized bedlam. Robert and his family arrived at the same time his brother and family. The kids couldn't wait to see Grandma and Grandpa's tree and what gifts awaited them under it.

Robert, however, was strangely quiet. At the first opportunity, he took his father aside.

"Do you remember that Christmas thirty years ago and the unwanted gift?" Robert asked.

"Come with me."

His father led Robert upstairs to the linen closet. He seemed to disappear under a mountain of towels and sheets and other household paraphernalia. When he emerged, there in his hands was the half-opened gift, just as Robert had left it.

---

[16] John 1:12, NIV.

"Here, son, open it."

That night, Robert couldn't sleep. He was in his old room, now a guest room, and he concluded that the gift wasn't all that bad after all. In fact, it was far better than the one he had obsessed about for months. It was something any ten-year-old boy would have loved! It just hadn't been what he had wanted and expected.

Robert quietly slipped out of bed, careful not to wake his wife, and went down to the living room. He plugged in the tree lights and sat in his father's favourite chair. With no one around, the tears began to flow.

"God, I've been pretty mean to You," he began. "I'm one of those people who, for many years, has refused to accept Your gift to me. Jesus has pretty much been unwanted in my life for a long time. Everything else around me seemed so much more exciting and fulfilling than going to church and following You. But now I realize that I've had it all wrong. I'm really not all that happy deep down inside. I get scared about things, like last year when the doctor found the spot on my liver. Thankfully it wasn't cancer, but it scared me. I didn't want to die. I didn't have anything to lean on. I didn't have anything to trust.

"And just two weeks ago, when the boss announced that the company was downsizing, I was worried. Those cuts usually begin in management. I could lose my job. God, nothing in this world is secure, is it? Only You. My unwanted, half-opened gift was still here after all those years. And just like the pastor said last night, You're still here too. It is not too late to receive Your Christmas gift to us.

"Lord, I know that Christmas can't be easy for You, what with having to give up Your Son while knowing that many people would mistreat Him. Well, God, I want to give You a gift this Christmas. I don't want Your gift to be unwanted in my life any longer. Lord, my present to You is me. It's not much, but it's all I have. I give You myself. I want to become one of Your children. I want the unwanted gift."

The Rescue

Brad loved Christmas. By mid-November, he was out on a ladder hanging Christmas lights from every part of the house he could hang lights on. Each year he found a way to add a few more to the display. He had Santa and snowmen and even a nativity scene that lit up. The nativity scene had been his wife's idea. He also loved Christmas music, so this year he'd added music.

Then two weeks before Christmas, it was off to the country with the family to cut their Christmas tree and bring it home. The tree had to be just a pinch under eight feet tall so it would touch the ceiling.

Decorating the tree had a liturgy all its own. The decorations had to adorn the tree in a particular order, and each person was assigned particular decorations to hang. Brad had choreographed each movement with military precision.

Then there were all the other Christmas traditions, including office parties. Brad even got to play Santa one year.

Yes, Brad really loved Christmas.

Well, he mostly loved Christmas. He just couldn't figure out why his wife Cynthia insisted on dragging him out every year to the Christmas Eve service at church. That was his least favourite part of the season. In fact, it was kind of depressing. Sure, there was the music, but all the talk about Jesus as Saviour got to Brad. What did a Saviour have to do with Santa or Christmas? If it was Saviour versus Santa, Santa would win every time, hands down.

He really didn't understand all the fuss about Jesus. That story was two thousand years old and had nothing to do with today.

"Brad, honey, wasn't that a wonderful service tonight?" Cynthia asked while they drove home from the service. She was always on top of the world after this yuletide ritual.

"Yeah, wonderful," he mumbled, barely audible.

The truth was that he'd found the Christmas Eve service particularly depressing. The new pastor hadn't just mentioned the dreaded word Saviour; he had dared to mention the other s-word. Sin. Instead of sticking to the traditional Christmas story, which at least Brad could tolerate, he'd referred to another story of the birth of Jesus.

The verse he'd used kept going around in Brad's mind. He couldn't get rid of it no matter how hard he tried. He tried thinking of all the important Christmas traditions that were special to him, but try as hard as he might, that verse kept coming back to him.

"She will give birth to a son and you are to give him the name Jesus because he will save his people from their sins."[17]

There it was again. He never gave a second thought to Bible verses, but this verse just wouldn't go away.

Christmas is probably ruined for me now, he brooded all the way home.

Once they were back, he busied himself by putting on a fire in the fireplace and then getting the cookies and milk ready for Santa. The kids loved this part of Christmas Eve and it made Brad feel that things were falling back into his comfort zone again.

"Brad, would you make a quick trip to the convenience store?" called his wife. "I just discovered what I forgot yesterday while shopping. We're nearly out of butter. And with the whole clan coming over tomorrow, I'll need lots."

"Sure. I'll be right back."

He put on his coat and boots. Maybe a trip to the store would fully clear his mind and get him back into the Christmas spirit.

The flurries that had been falling earlier were now much heavier and the snow was accumulating on the road.

---

[17] Matthew 1:21, NIV.

I'll just shift into four-wheel drive and be home in no time, he thought as he eased out onto the street.

It all happened so fast, and Brad had a front row seat. He was stopped at a red light when right before his eyes a car came up on his right and tried to make a right turn, but the wheels hit a patch of ice that sent the car speeding through the intersection sideways and right into a light post.

At first Brad couldn't move. It played out all like a bad dream, but without thinking he then jumped out of his car and ran across the street. As he ran toward the crumpled car, he noticed a flicker of flame under the hood.

All Brad could think of was, *I have to get this person out of the car or they might die.*

As he neared the car, he realized that the driver's door had struck the light post. It was bashed in about a foot and the driver was slumped awkwardly over the bent steering wheel, his head resting on the dashboard. No way could that door be opened.

He went around to the passenger door, which opened easily. That's when he got his first look at the injured driver. What he saw made him stop. It was Barry Meyer.

Brad froze. Part of him wanted to just run back to his vehicle and drive off, pretending he hadn't seen anything.

Barry Meyer, of all people, he thought. *The little weasel.*

When the regional management position had come open last summer, Brad had known he was shoe-in. He had the experience and had all but been promised the next promotion. But he'd been blindsided by Barry's betrayal.

At the job interview, Brad went for what he thought was the mandatory, but routine interview, kind of going through the motions then he would receive the promotion, but routine it wasn't. Right from the get-go, something didn't seem right. The interviewer—the usual amiable Alex—wasn't his usual jovial self. His smile was replaced by an all-business expression.

As soon as Alex asked his first question, Brad knew he was dead meat.

"So why didn't you ever tell us you stole a car?" Alex asked.

Brad felt like he had been kicked in the stomach. All the wind went out of his lungs and he felt like he was suffocating. Big drops of sweat broke out on his forehead.

"You never indicated anything about that of your applications or subsequence interviews," Alex said, relentlessly.

Brad couldn't say a word. He opened his mouth but nothing came out.

"Brad, I can't say how disappointed I am. You're the best accountant we have by far, and this position would be a perfect fit for you, but I'm offering it to Barry Meyer."

The interview was over.

Brad sat in the boardroom for a full fifteen minutes before he went back to his desk. He'd half-expected his stuff to be packed up and accompanied by a pink slip, but everything was just as he had left it.

That was the only bit of relief Brad felt all day. For the next several days, actually.

How had Alex found out? Only his parents and best friend at the time had known anything of this story. It had happened twenty-four years ago when he was fifteen. Ken had dared him to take his parents' car for a drive around the block. Well, long story short, he had accepted the dare, but the block turned out to be several blocks. One too many. On that last block, the police pulled him over. No charges were laid; sitting in the back of a police cruiser in handcuffs waiting for his parents had been punishment enough.

So who squealed?

Then it dawned on him. A couple of years ago, Ken had hit the big city and dropped by the office. But before Brad had been able to get away to meet him for lunch, he'd had to tidy up a few loose ends. He'd noticed Barry talking to Ken, who must have spilled the beans in one of those you-should-have-known-Brad-in-his-wilder-days kind of conversations. He must have used this bit of information to sabotage Brad's promotion.

Brad had vowed never to talk to Barry again, and he hadn't. But now the one who had betrayed him was out cold with possibly serious injuries in a car that was ready to burn. He could drive off and no one would know he had ever been there. The streets were empty.

He couldn't let another human being die, though, no matter who that person was or what he had done.

Brad unfastened Barry's seatbelt and tried to lift him up and out, but he couldn't budge him. Smoke was starting to fill the car and it was getting hot.

Brad felt a sharp pain on his right hand. A flame was visible through the heating vent. He pulled again, and this time Barry moved, but only slightly.

With one more pull, the whole weight of Barry's body fell against Brad, nearly pushing him out the door of the car. He glanced at his right arm and saw that his coat and shirt on that side had burned away.

Barry came out with one last pull. He landed on top of Brad as they tumbled onto the street. In more pain than he had ever experienced, Brad looked up into the face of a stranger on their cell. Everything went black.

* * *

When Brad awoke, his clothes had been replaced by a hospital gown and the searing hot pain on his right side was unbearable. A nurse came into the room.

"What time is it?" he asked.

"It's 11:20 on Christmas morning."

He had missed Christmas morning with his wife and kids, including all the presents and traditions. Why?

Then it came back to him—Barry Meyer, the crash, getting him out of the car…

"How's Barry?" As soon as the question came out of his mouth, Brad couldn't believe he had asked it. Why should he care after all Barry had done to him.

But he did care. For some strange reason, he hoped Barry wasn't dead.

"You mean the man you rescued?" the nurse asked.

"Yes."

"Mr. Meyer is going to be okay. He has a concussion, and a broken arm and collar bone. He's very fortunate you came along when you did or he wouldn't have lived. From what the news is reporting, you saved his life. The car burned completely before the fire truck got there. You'll be able to see him soon, but first I have to change the dressings on your hand and arm."

For the first time, Brad noticed his right hand and arm wrapped in heavy white bandages.

"You have second degree burns to your right hand and arm," she continued. "You'll be here for a few days. There will be some scarring, but you should be good in three to four months."

Three to four months! I thought. *Merry Christmas to me.*

"Your wife was here overnight with you," said the nurse. "She'll be back by 2:00 p.m. She wanted to see the kids and explain what had happened. Let them know their father is a hero."

Three to four months... and Barry would likely walk out of here in three to four days, good as new.

The nurse was gone now.

He remembered the verse again, from the Christmas Eve service: *"She will give birth to a son and you are to give him the name Jesus because he will save his people from their sins."*[18] The words just popped right into his mind like a giant billboard in front of his eyes.

"Way to go, mister!" A man in a white lab coat was standing by the door, giving Brad two thumbs up. He must have been a doctor. "Great job. You saved a man's life."

This was all too strange. It was Christmas Eve and he had saved the life of a man he had wished dead for what he had done. And now Brad was paying the price for that rescue. A very painful price.

Cynthia spent the afternoon with Brad. She explained that his sister had volunteered to do the cooking at home. Cynthia planned to pop home just long enough to eat, then get right back to the hospital.

"No, really, you don't need to come back tonight," Brad interjected. "I'm fine. Besides, the kids need you at home."

"Are you sure?"

---

[18] Matthew 1:21, NIV.

Brad needed some time to think. "Positive."

"Okay, but I'll be here bright and early tomorrow morning."

Christmas dinner was served in a bag and delivered by needle. After that, the ward quieted down. Earlier in the evening all the hospital staff and two fireman had come by to thank him for a job well done.

That verse had kept coming back into his head. Could this really be what Christmas was all about? Was there more to Christmas than lights and trees and Santa and presents? Wasn't this what his wife had been trying to tell him?

We were on a course that would cause us to crash and burn, he thought. *That is, until Jesus came to earth to rescue us, to be our Saviour. Our sins set us on this course...*

All this heavy duty thinking made Brad sleepy. Soon he nodded off.

* * *

Brad didn't see the other vehicle until it was too late. He had only glanced at his phone for a moment when he heard the familiar notification. But that moment was all it took for Brad to drive through a red light. Brad, who never did anything wrong.

Hit dead-on by a dump truck, Brad's SUV crumpled in seconds. All Brad felt was a searing pain over his whole body. Then there was silence and everything went black.

He hovered over his wrecked car, looking in. He saw his twisted body, his head lying on what was left of the passenger's seat. Flames were starting to flicker from under the dash.

As Brad regained conscious, he realized that he had to get out, but he couldn't move. He is trapped in a car about to burn and maybe even explode. Then Brad saw him; he wasn't alone. He had never seen this stranger before, but he knew exactly who it was.

When the stranger spoke, his voice was strong and reassuring: "I got this."

Brad watched as the stranger wrapped his arms around him. As he did so, Brad noticed scars on the palms of his hands. Gently this stranger lifted him and carried him right out of the smouldering wreck. They had just made it a safe distance when the vehicle exploded in a ball of fire…

* * *

Brad awoke in a full sweat. His hospital gown was soaked and the sheets were wet. It had been a dream, but it had felt so real!

Suddenly, Brad realized that he wasn't alone. There, standing at the end of the bed, was Barry.

"You probably don't want to talk to me, or even see me," Barry said. "I wouldn't blame you one bit. But I just have to say thank you. Thank you for saving my life. I would really like the opportunity to talk with you, but now's not the time. There's a lot I need to say."

Brad looked up from his pillow. "I would welcome the opportunity to talk. In a roundabout way, you've been a big help in saving my life as well."

Boxing Day

"I hate Boxing Day."

That was the first thought to run through Andrew's mind when he woke up on December 26. The feeling was the same every year. At about 10:00 p.m. on Christmas Day, Andrew began to feel sad as a sense of despair entered his heart. He would try to push it back, but by the next morning he would be lost in depression. Christmas was over, gone. It was like saying goodbye to someone you really love and won't see them for another whole year.

Andrew loved Christmas. For the six weeks leading up to December 25, he got really into the holiday. First there were the lights and decorations. Then came the writing of Christmas cards, not to mention receiving them.

On the second week of December, he and his wife always drove out to a tree farm, but not to get a pre-cut tree. No siree. They always cut their own tree and brought it home on the roof of the car. And over the next couple of days, they decorated that tree until it was just perfect.

Next came the buying of gifts. He didn't want to do it too early, in case something new came out later that he just had to buy. He didn't care much about himself and what he got—but, please, no ties. What he really enjoyed was watching the faces of the family as they each opened the special gifts he had purchased. He spent a lot of time picking out these gifts. They had to be items he knew they wouldn't get for themselves because it was just too extravagant. He would never forget the look on his daughter's face the year she had opened her gift to discover the very expensive watch she had been wanting for a very long time. Her face just lit up.

Now that he had grandchildren, he enjoyed the same thing. He loved seeing their beaming faces when they opened their gifts. Their smiles and laughter were priceless.

But now it was Boxing Day and Christmas was over for another whole year. In a few hours, Andrew's son and daughter and their families would be packing up their cars and heading home. He wouldn't see his son and family until next Christmas. At least his daughter made a point to come by with her two children for a few hours on his birthday, but that was it. Everyone was so busy.

The tree was beginning to lose its needles and his wife would be after him to get that messy thing out of the living room before every room in the house was bristling with needles.

The peace and goodwill of Christmas had been replaced by people pushing and shoving for Boxing Day sales. As if they hadn't gotten enough, or hadn't gotten what they really wanted.

And the world? Children were still dying, refugee camps were still filled to capacity, car bombs were going off, dictators dictated, and governments fought amongst themselves for their own survival rather than caring for the people who had elected them. The women's shelters were no less crowded. There were still stalkings and shootings and gang wars. Divorce court was just as busy as ever, and so was the Children's Aid Society.

So what difference did Christmas really make?

It's just the same old, same old, thought Andrew. *Only it seems worse now, after all the caring and charitable giving and emotional high of Christmas.*

With the lights of Christmas extinguished, the world seemed even darker than ever.

All morning, Andrew moped around the house, and in the afternoon his wife went out shopping. "It's a good time to get birthday presents for the grandkids," she'd told him. "Can't beat the sales.'

Andrew settled in on the sofa and decided to read a bit. That didn't last long. Soon he was fast asleep.

He awoke with a start.

"Who turned on the TV?" he asked no one in particular. He reached for the remote and pushed the off button, but nothing happened. He tried again, but nothing happened.

He got up and tried using the on/off switch. Still, the TV stayed on.

Andrew pulled the plug, but the TV still blared away, advertising some drug whose side effects would be worse than the problem it was intended to relieve.

As he stood there trying to figure out what to do next, he heard his name.

"Andrew, over here. Andrew."

The voice was coming from the TV. The commercial was over and a man stood right in the middle of the screen. Someone he had never seen before, yet he looked like...

He couldn't believe it. But the man looked like one of the shepherds who was part of the annual Sunday school Christmas pageant. This shepherd was far more authentic, though. There was no bathrobe or towel for this guy. He was the real deal, or so it seemed.

"Who are you?" Andrew asked.

Oh great, he thought. *Now I'm talking to a shepherd on my TV...*

"I'm a shepherd," the man replied. "You know, one of those who was around the night Jesus was born. Out in the fields, watching over my flocks by night. Angels... the heavenly chorus... you know, the whole routine. I was there."

"You were?"

"I was." He nodded. "I saw the baby Jesus face to face in Bethlehem that night."

"You did?"

"I did. I looked on the face of God that night. And you know what? I haven't been the same since. Jesus turned everything around in my life."

"He did?"

"He did. I used to go to synagogue when I could, but work often got in the way. I attended all the sacred services, but it didn't do much good. My mind would wander. I thought about work and what I would do on my days off. I heard the teacher, but it was just words. God was far from me. Or more correctly, I was far from God. He was just some mythological figure I had grown up hearing about but never taken seriously. I liked the stories about whales swallowing people and walls falling down at the sound of a trumpet and giants being killed by a young shepherd... but they were only stories. No way could they be true. To be honest, worship was a bore, a lot of gobbledygook. It made no real sense to me. It didn't seem relevant at all."

Andrew could relate. "That's exactly how I feel about going to church. I've been going all my life, but it means very little to me..."

He stopped midsentence. What was he doing talking to a two-thousand-year-old shepherd on his TV?

"Andrew, have you seen the face of God?" the shepherd asked. "Have you ever felt His presence?"

"No, not like you. You got to see Jesus in person."

"I know, but after that experience I began to meet God all the time. Going to worship was never the same. As the Holy Scriptures were read, it was as if God was reading to me. And prayer? After that night in Bethlehem, I no longer mouthed the words thinking that I was talking to some mythological concept. My prayers are directed to a real being, a real person. I now know that God is listening. I can even hear Him speak back to me. He plants thoughts in my mind and feelings in my heart. He even directs my attention to particular words in Scripture. I know you don't think my experience in Bethlehem makes any difference. To you, it may just seem the same old thing, but it does make a difference. It made a difference to me! But only after I changed my attitude toward God. Jesus didn't come as a social activist to change the world. He came as a Saviour to change our hearts."

With that, the shepherd faded from view. Andrew drew a deep breath and sat back as the screen went black. "Whew!" he said aloud. "I'm glad that's over."

"Not so fast, Andrew."

"Who said that?" Andrew looked back to the TV and saw another man on the screen. This man was in his late fifties, or maybe early sixties. He had long curly hair and was dressed like a clergyman from Victorian England. The man even spoke with an English accent.

Andrew sat up on the edge of his chair. "Who are you?"

"Newton's the name. John Newton. You don't know me, but you do know some of the hymns I've written."

"I do?"

"You sure do. You can't tell me you've never sung 'Amazing Grace.'"

"That one I do know. It's the one hymn we sing that really chokes me up. I don't let on, of course, but when we sing those lyrics it's as if I can hear God talking directly to me. I can feel it in my heart. It's pretty amazing. But then, you already know that, don't you?"

"It had the same effect on me when God gave me those words," Newton agreed. "They describe my life, you know. I wasn't always a saint, and I sure didn't choose to be a minister. I was captain of a ship and a pretty rough character. Early on, I got involved in the slave trade. I'd take a shipload of goods to a port in Africa where indigenous people were rounded up and held. I'd offload my cargo and then fill up the boat with slaves and deliver them to England or the Americas."

"You were a slave trader?"

"Well, not technically. But I did provide the transportation."

Andrew stopped for a minute to take in what was happening. He was carrying on a conversation with an eighteenth-century minister.

He scratched his head. *Oh well,* he thought. *I've already talked to a two-thousand-year-old shepherd. At least we're getting more recent.*

"So what made the difference in your life?" Andrew asked.

"God did. That little baby born in the stable in Bethlehem."

There seemed to be a lot of that going around.

"On one of my voyages, we were nearing home and a huge storm hit," Newton continued. "The ship began taking on water and I got scared. I prayed, as I'd seen my mother do when I was a child. I told God that if He rescued me, I would become one of His followers. Well, we made it and I kept my promise. I gave my heart to the Lord. That's when things began to change for me. Not overnight necessarily, but slowly

God worked on my heart. Over time I surrendered more and more of my life to Jesus."

"You gave control of your life to God?"

"I certainly did, and I can tell you that there will be no difference in your life until you completely turn it over to God."

Andrew narrowed his eyes. "You're not talking about a personal faith, are you? That kind of talk scares me. It's too… too… well, it's too personal. The shepherd told me the same thing. He talked about Jesus being a Saviour, not of the world but for me personally."

"He's right, Andrew. God showed me that in my heart I was dying. In some ways, I was even dead. In the Bible, Paul gives us a before and after picture. First he writes, 'As for you, you were dead in your transgressions and sins in which you used to live.'[19] But he follows that up with this good news: 'But because of His great love for us, God in His rich mercy made us alive with Christ and this by grace.'"[20]

Andrew's head was swimming. Dead… alive… a personal faith… a relationship with God…? He had always thought church was about doing things, about performing good deeds and making a difference in the community and the world. It wasn't about all this other stuff.

"Andrew, keep up here, will you? I'm losing you."

"Yeah, sure, Mr. Newton. I'm here."

"Have you heard of the Bible verse, John 3:16?" Newton asked.

"I have."

"Do you know what it says?"

"I looked it up once. It says something about God loving us and giving us His only Son so wouldn't perish but have eternal life."

"Exactly."

"Exactly what?" Andrew sighed. "Oh, I get it. More talk about death and life."

"Exactly."

"Hey, Mr. Newton, you've been dead for more than two hundred years, yet here I am talking to you. What gives? And that's not a trivial question."

---

[19] Ephesians 2:1, NIV.
[20] Ephesians 2:4, NIV.

"No, actually it isn't a trivial question. It's a very good question. But you probably will have trouble with my answer."

"I will?"

"You will."

"I will." Andrew almost sounded convinced.

"You see, I may not be alive here on the earth, but I'm not dead either."

"You're not? I mean, of course you're not. Why would I ever think a two-hundred-year-old man wasn't dead…"

"Because I'm not dead."

Andrew nodded along. "Wait a minute. Jesus came as our Saviour, our personal Saviour, and He came to change hearts and make a difference personally so we could go to heaven when we die. Next you're going to tell me that Easter plays a role in all this. Well, I have to tell you: I'm not big on Easter. It just doesn't have the same appeal as Christmas. I mean, how can you even compare a story about a cute baby with an execution by crucifixion? It's all so depressing. And it most certainly doesn't lend itself to blow-up characters on the front lawn and bright twinkling lights."

"You're right, Andrew. Easter is about death. But it's also about life. Don't forget the best part: the empty tomb. Death ended that day. That's the biggest change of all. In that little baby in the manger, you have the difference between life and death. You also have the secret about how to change the world."

"How's that?"

"Andrew, do you know the rest of my story?"

"No, not really."

"Well, as God worked on my heart and changed me, He caused an absolute hatred for the slave trade to grow within me. The very activity I used to make my living at, and a very good living it was, I now totally despised. One day a member of the British parliament, a man by the name of William Wilberforce, came to see me. He was trying to get legislation passed to end the slave trade, but he was tired of all the opposition to his proposal. I was able to encourage him to press forward. He did, and he got the legislation passed that banned slavery."

Andrew smiled. "That's amazing. What a difference that made in so many thousands of people's lives! And all because of a change God made in your life. Imagine… a former slave trader responsible for ending slavery, or at least making a huge contribution to ending it…"

"That's right, Andrew, and it never would have happened if God hadn't first changed my heart and made a difference in me. All those things you associate with Christmas, they aren't able to change anything in our lives, our community, or our world. Tinsel, trees, and traditions… they're all window dressing. It's the baby born in the manger that makes the difference, first in us and then, as God works through us, to the community and the world."

Andrew sat back in his chair as the TV went black.

Suddenly, he heard his wife come in through the back door. "Andrew, can you come out to the car and help me with these parcels?"

Andrew opened his eyes. His book had fallen to the floor. In his heart, for the very first time ever, he felt genuine hope, not despair. The cloud that had hung over his head was gone. The sadness he had felt an hour or so ago had been replaced with joy. Real joy. He felt better than he ever had while hanging Christmas lights, decorating the tree, or buying the presents.

He felt as if he had been dead but was now alive. Where had he heard those words? They seemed strangely familiar to him.

Then he remembered his two visitors.

Andrew closed his eyes. "God, I don't really know what I'm doing yet, but I want that baby born in Bethlehem to be born in my heart. I want to get to know You personally. I want that baby to make difference in my life."

His prayer was interrupted by his wife, loaded down with shopping bags, standing at the entrance to the living room. "Andrew, what in heaven's name are you doing?"

And Andrew answered, "Exactly."

The Gift Revisited[21]

The loud crack was followed immediately by a sharp pain in Owen's chest as he fell backwards to the mall floor. He knew he had been shot and would be dead in a matter of minutes.

A surge of fear and sadness washed over him. It wasn't supposed to end like this. He had plans. Big plans. He wanted to see his kids graduate from high school. He wanted to walk his daughter down the aisle at her wedding. He wanted to have playdates with his grandchildren. He wanted to spend his entire summers with Maria at the trailer when he retired. Two weeks a year wasn't enough. Now he would have none of these experiences.

He closed his eyes and wondered what death would be like.

But Owen didn't die. The cold mall floor was not to be his final resting place. Five minutes after the loud crack of the gun, he either was still alive or the other side of death was very much like the side he had just left.

As the pain in his chest subsided, he tried to sit up. Lo and behold, no problem. Next he tried to stand, and in no time he was on his feet. With a quick look around, everything came into focus. Right in the centre of his vest was a wicked tear around a small hole filled with a small-calibre bullet. A bullet meant for his heart.

---

[21] This story had its beginnings in a news article I read second- or third-hand several years ago. It was the story of a person receiving a bulletproof vest as a Christmas present and how this vest saved the recipient's life. I have taken the concept of this article and fictionalized it.

The events of the past few minutes began to sink in. It had been late. The mall was closed. He'd been doing his routine security rounds. Nothing ever happened here.

But now it had.

Now that he was reasonably sure he wouldn't die, Owen called 911—and while talking to the emergency operator he noted the sliding door on the jewellery store across the hall. It had been broken open, but no one seemed to be inside. Not now anyway.

That's when it dawned on Owen. What if the shooter was still in the mall? Fear gripped his heart. He might still be a target.

There were sirens, lots of sirens, as the 911 operator had connected Owen to one of the responding officers.

"Sir, sir, are you in a safe place?"

"I can hide in a store."

"Good. Just tell us which one. And no lights."

"I'll be in 'Take a Spin,' the retro vinyl record store."

"Got it."

Owen moved as quietly and quickly as possible to the music store just down the hall from where he'd been standing. He slipped his universal key in the lock. Once inside, he made his way to the back of the store, using the flashlight on his phone. In his haste, he nearly knocked over a rack of Neil Diamond CDs.

Song Sung Blue, he thought. *That's for sure...*

He slumped down behind a shelf of videos, his heart still pounding as his thoughts bounced off the inside of his skull. He had been shot and lived to tell about it, at least so far. And it was all thanks to the Christmas gift his wife had given him less than four months ago.

Two days before Christmas, Maria had placed a large wrapped present under the tree, a present with Owen's name on it. This had been completely unexpected and not really welcome. Owen and Maria had decided several years ago to combine their resources and rent a trailer for two weeks on a lake up north each summer. This was to be their Christmas gift to each other. And this plan had worked really well, until now.

Owen was annoyed with his beloved. She had apparently broken the rules. And now what was he to do? Should he go and look for a gift for her? He decided not to do so. If Maria was going to break the rules, that would be on her. He would stick to their no-gifts policy.

Christmas morning came and Owen grew even more annoyed. After being presented with the gift and instructed to open it, Owen discovered that his dear wife had given him a bulletproof vest. Maria had been after him to get one for some time. The security company didn't provide them at work, and she was fearful he'd need it one day.

"It's always better to be safe than sorry," she said.

How many times had Owen heard those words over the past few years?

He'd made all kinds of excuses for not getting a vest. None of the other guys at work wore one. If no one else thought it was important, neither would he.

Besides, his wife was making a mountain out of a molehill. He worked in the local mall and it wasn't the big bad city. Nothing bad ever happened. There was no threat of real danger. The most excitement he ever encountered was catching a shoplifter.

Maria had taken this vest thing to the next level. He wasn't happy.

For three months, Owen had refused to wear the vest. Then, about four weeks ago, he had softened and told his wife he would wear it once and a while, when he felt like it. Tonight, for some reason, he had felt like it. He was going to have to swallow his pride and thank Maria for the gift.

Owen heard a key in the lock at the front of the store. A minute or two later, the lights came on.

"Owen!" It was his boss, Jacob. He would recognize that voice anywhere. "Owen! You in here?"

Owen made his way to the front of the store where two uniformed officers were waiting outside with Jacob and a pair of paramedics.

"Are you okay?" Jacob's voice was shaky.

Jacob was the best boss Owen had ever worked for. He genuinely cared for each of his employees.

"I'm fine," Owen said. "A bit of a sore chest."

"Let the paramedics check you out. Then, if you're okay, the officers need to get a statement."

One of the officers spoke up. "Before you take off that vest, we would like to take a picture of it on you."

"Go ahead."

A special police issue camera appeared and several pictures were taken.

The paramedics completed their examination of his chest and checked his vital signs.

"You're one blessed man, Mr. Salazar," said one of the paramedics. "By the location of the hole in your vest, that bullet was headed for your left ventricle. Without your vest, you wouldn't be here right now. As it is, you'll have a pretty good bruise on your chest for a few days, but it will heal. Do you want to go to the hospital for a more thorough checkup?"

"No, I'm good."

"If you feel like anything's wrong, don't wait. Go directly to the hospital. We can't tell for sure how deep that bruise is."

"I'm fine. Thanks."

Once Owen had finished giving the officers his recollections of what had happened and answered their questions, Jacob told him to just go on home; he would finish up things at the mall.

Once outside, Owen found the fresh air invigorating. It helped to clear his mind.

He just sat in his car for a few minutes before heading home. Now he would have to explain all this to Maria. He had texted her while hiding in the music store to tell her that he'd be a little late. He'd explained that there'd been an incident at the mall, but not to worry.

When he got home and told her everything, she reacted exactly the way he had expected.

"An incident! Not to worry! I could have become a widow tonight."

After this understandable outburst, Maria wrapped her arms around him and held on forever. But what was missing from his wife's reaction? "I told you so."

In fact, all Maria said was, "I'm thankful to our heavenly Father that you're okay. Now I'm going to bed. Are you coming?"

"I'll be there in a few minutes."

Once Maria had left the room, Owen took a can of cola from the fridge and sat in his living room chair. When he cracked open the can, he jumped. With a long draw of the cold, fizzy beverage, Owen fell asleep in his chair.

When he awoke, he was no longer in his chair—or even in his living room. Owen found himself in a college dormitory. The same dorm room where he'd spent his first year away at school.

He watched as his mom and dad got ready to leave after helping him move in.

After a bit of an awkward silence, his dad spoke. "We're always here for you. We love you and wish the very best for you."

"Son, would you please find a good church and connect with it?" Mom asked.

Dad rolled his eyes and looked up at the ceiling.

"Mom, you know I'm not all that big on church," Owen said. "I really don't see the need of it. It's not like I'm going to die anytime soon. Besides, no one else my age goes to church."

She looked lovingly at me, but with sadness in her eyes. Owen really didn't want to hurt her.

"I'll make an effort to find a church and go once in a while," he said at last. "When I feel the need."

Owen didn't like where this was all going.

When the second scene arrived, the air was sweet and cool, but not too cool. The sun shone brightly, but not too brightly. The garden path was lined on both sides with the most beautiful flowers Owen had ever seen. Birds of every size and colour danced in the sunlight, flitting and floating on the breeze while singing the most beautiful songs.

As he explored this delightful garden, Owen was quite taken aback to see a lion lying in the grass alongside a lamb. What kind of place was this?

Suddenly, Owen heard voices—two voices, to be exact. A few more steps and there, sitting on a bench, were two men engaged in a lively chitchat.

"It all happened so quickly," one man said to the other. "I heard the holdup alarm go off, activated by one of the tellers. I left my office to see if I could help diffuse the situation. As I entered the hallway, I saw a man waving a gun around and shouting orders. He had a large backpack and wanted it filled with money. As one of the tellers moved to honour his request, he pointed the gun right at her. 'Don't!' I instinctively shouted. And he turned around and fired in my direction. A few moments later, I was here."

Owen came to a stop immediately in front of these two men, but they apparently couldn't see him.

"I don't recall any pain or fear," the man continued. "The first thing I felt was someone taking my hand and walking with me away from the earth. My eyes slowly moved up from the floor and I looked into the most beautiful face I had ever seen, the face of Jesus. His voice was calm as He assured me that He was taking me to my home in His Father's house. A deep, deep peace filled my entire being."

The other gentleman nodded, smiling. "I know the feeling. One minute I was lying in a hospital bed and the next Jesus took my hand and led me right here."

The first speaker returned to his story. "I'm so glad I stopped being stubborn, making excuses not to become a follower of Jesus. I used to hate all the religious stuff, and the worst was Christmas Eve. My wife always insisted that the entire family, myself included, go to church. Now, don't get me wrong. I loved Christmas. It was the best time of year. Who doesn't like all the lights and decorations? My outdoor display won first prize every year. And what about the music? 'Silver Bells,' 'White Christmas,' the list could go on and on. Then there's the tree, colourful lights twinkling and covered in special ornaments. On Christmas Eve, I just wanted to sit in the dark with the tree lights on. It was so beautiful.

"I didn't want to go to some church service and be preached at. It just ruined the atmosphere. Who needed Jesus? My life was just fine without Him. I was young, healthy, and everything was good. I had a great job and lots of leisure time. I couldn't see any danger on the horizon. Besides, none of the other guys I hung around with went to church and they all seemed to be doing real well. I certainly didn't want to be the odd man out. As far as I could see, getting all wrapped up in that Christian stuff would be a burden, dragging me down and killing the mood.

"But to keep the peace in the family, I grudgingly accompanied my wife and kids to the Christmas Eve service. This year, I was in a particularly grumpy mood. I just didn't want to be subjected to all the religious baggage I knew would be coming my way. I endured the first part of the service, but just barely. I wasn't sure if I could make it to the end. I knew there was a sermon coming and couldn't stand the idea of someone preaching at me. Not that night, not ever.

"Then something quite remarkable happened. The pastor began his message with words I hadn't seen coming: 'How many people wish they weren't here tonight? How many folk wish they were anywhere else but here?' All of a sudden he had my attention. It was like he had climbed into my head."

"The pastor continued, 'No, I don't expect you to raise your hand, but I do know that some are only present because you didn't feel you had a choice. I know this because I was one of you a few years ago. The world gave me all the Christmas I could ever want. I certainly didn't need Jesus. In fact, including Him in my life felt more like a burden than a blessing. It would hold me back from doing what I wanted. My friends might think I wasn't strong, that I couldn't handle life on my own. I didn't want to lose popularity. The original Christmas gift was one I was quite sure I could do without.

"'Until I wasn't so sure anymore. In my last year at university, I was driving home for Christmas on a dark and snowy night. All of a sudden, the headlights of a transport truck appeared in my lane, approaching fast. I swerved, went through the ditch, and hit a tree. Now I had to think about death. It was pending—now.

"'But somehow I survived. The paramedics couldn't believe it when they cut me out of the wreck. I had very serious injuries, and it's why I walk with a limp, but I dodged a bullet that night.'

"The pastor's words struck a chord with me. These were words I could no longer ignore, especially when he went on to explain that he'd realized he could no longer ignore the gift of Christmas. He needed to revisit that gift in all its glory and life-changing power. Now he saw

Jesus not as a superfluous addition to Christmas, but as the very heart of Christmas. The other ornaments we attach to this holy holiday are the superficial additions, human inventions we use to try satisfying the deep longings of the heart. But only Jesus has the ability to really meet our deepest needs. The world and its artificial pacifiers can't do what Jesus did. He came to bear our sins when He died on the cross and then rose from the dead three days later."

The storyteller paused, as if hearing the pastor's words all over again. Once he had collected his thoughts, he carried on.

"I no longer felt invincible. In fact, I realized just how fragile and temporary life is. The pastor awoke in me a deep need in my heart I had been ignoring. That night, I whispered a quiet prayer, confessing my sins, especially of arrogance. I then committed my life to Jesus Christ. I couldn't ignore the gift of Christmas any longer.

"Well, that was just over three months ago. Can you believe that? Three months ago, I became a follower of Jesus. And now here I am, escorted by my Saviour into our heavenly Father's eternal home. When that bullet came at me, death was taking its best shot. But it lost. I was shielded from its sting by Jesus. He was my bulletproof vest."

Suddenly, Owen awoke. He was still sitting in his favourite chair. He reached out instinctively for his cola and found that it was still ice cold.

He took a long drink and headed up to bed, but not to sleep. His mind was overwhelmed with thoughts he would never have imagined having before. His heart was bursting with feelings that were both troubling and comforting.

He finally fell into a fitful sleep around 5:00 a.m.

Three hours later, he entered the kitchen where Maria was preparing breakfast for herself.

She spoke first. "I'm sorry. I tried to be quiet so you could sleep."

"Maria, I'm coming to the Good Friday service with you today. I want the gift of Christmas."

The Good Shepherd

"Mother, please, you've got to let me go."

"I don't got to let you do anything. I said no and that's what I meant. No. Understand?"

"It's only for one night, and Uncle Aaron will be right there the whole time. Nothing will happen to me."

"I said no."

There was a knock at the door, but before I could get across the room to open it Uncle Aaron had let himself in.

"So what's all the commotion in here?" he said. "I could hear you across the lane and right into my backyard. Come on, Abigail, let the boy come out with us tonight. It's going to be a quiet night. It'll be a good night for Simon to get his feet wet. He's got to start somewhere."

Mother turned back to me. "Simon, you go to your room. Your hard-headed uncle and I have some talking to do."

I knew when it was time to make myself scarce. I headed to the back room but didn't close the door all the way. Uncle Aaron could be as stubborn as Mother. And when she said there was talking to do, it could be pretty entertaining.

Mother started. "What's wrong with you, coming around here like this and interfering? I'm Simon's mother. I've said no and that's what I mean."

"But, Abigail, it's only for one night. It's one of the quietest times of the year. I'll keep him by my side."

"One night is all it takes. It was a night just like this, supposedly the quiet time of the year, when he kissed me goodbye. It happened right there where you're standing. He told me he'd see me in the morning. But he didn't me see in the morning, did he? He never came home. You had to come in the middle of the night to tell me my husband had been killed by wolves, and why? He was protecting a bunch of sheep. That's all. Sheep. My husband, my boy's father, your brother, died protecting a bunch of sheep. A human life lost so some sheep could live. It hardly seems fair, does it? God's not fair. He took my husband from me. Well, He's not going to take my son too."

"But Abigail—"

"Before you say anything, Aaron, don't think I don't appreciate everything you've done for us. Letting us stay here in your cottage was especially a blessing. I don't know what I would have done without everything you and Dorcas have done for us. But you can't have my son tonight or any night."

"I hear everything you're saying. Not a day goes by that I don't miss my brother, but we have to be realistic. Simon will be thirteen on his next birthday. He has to learn a trade, and the only trade our family knows is shepherding. My father was a shepherd and his father before him was a shepherd. We could probably trace our roots all the way back to Abel. It's an honest job. I know most people look down on us. I've heard what they say—'You always smell bad. You're all crooks.' And I know we never get invited to the special events around town. 'They're just shepherds,' people say. But I'm proud of being a shepherd. Sheep need us. And the people? Even the people in their fancy homes who have fancy parties? They love to eat the meat, and they make their special clothes out of the wool. And do you know what makes me feel most proud? When one of the flock is chosen to be the sacrificial lamb. It has to be a firstborn, without blemish. What an honour to know that I've taken care of the very lamb that will be offered to Almighty God so our sins can be forgiven! It makes me feel as if somehow I'm a little closer to God."

"It's one thing for a sheep to give up its life so a shepherd can be forgiven. Or anyone else, for that matter," Mother said. "But it's quite another thing when a shepherd gives up his life for a sheep. Where's the justice in that?"

"Dear Abigail, remember the words of our great ancestor, David, who wrote those simple yet beautiful words, 'The Lord is my shepherd.' And remember how he talked of God protecting us in all the circumstances of life. Even in the presence of our enemies, Almighty God has promised to be there for us. If He were a real shepherd, He would be willing to give up His life for His sheep, even you and I."

Mother was quiet for a few minutes. "If God is such a good shepherd, why didn't He protect my Nathan? Aaron, it's getting late. Time for you to go."

And so without another word, Mother ushered Uncle Aaron out the door. This meant I was in for the night.

Or so I thought. I had been asleep for some time when I suddenly heard such a banging on the door that I thought the world was coming to an end.

"Wake up! Abigail, Simon... wake up!"

It was Uncle Aaron. I opened my eyes to see that it was still dark, long before sunrise. I heard Mother make her way to the door. When she opened it, there stood Uncle Aaron, lamp in hand.

"Simon, Abigail... you've got to come with me. You won't believe it. It's incredible. Guess who we saw?" He spoke through gulps of breath. He must have run all the way from the fields. "There were angels and... oh, you won't believe me. Just come."

"Where?" It was the only word my mother could get out of her mouth.

"Down to the old inn by the town gate."

Mother turned to me. "Simon, get dressed and go with your uncle. See what all the fuss is all about. I'm too tired. Just be sure this isn't a trick to get you out into the fields."

"I promise it's no trick," Uncle Aaron insisted. "This is the real thing."

I quickly got dressed and left with him. I could hardly keep up. It was dark, very dark, except for a few homes where lamps were being lit because other crazy shepherds had awakened other sleeping families.

When we got to the inn, we didn't go in through the front door but rather made our way down the laneway and through the back gate. We ran across the courtyard and entered the stable where the animals of the travellers were bedded down.

Instead of dark and quiet, the stable was alive with light and sound. Down past one row of stalls, we turned a corner and came upon a sight unlike anything I'd ever seen. There in one of the larger stalls was a young family. The father looked down at the source of this whole delightful commotion: a beautiful newborn baby, lying in the manger. The mother was leaning against some straw, also staring at her son.

The world seemed to stand still and go completely silent. All the noise of the awakened animals disappeared. Other shepherds gathered around, and though their mouths were moving I heard no sound.

It was as if it was just me and the baby. I looked at his face as peace filled my heart.

Uncle Aaron had snuck up behind me and spoke in a whisper. "It's the Messiah, Simon. That baby. He's the Messiah. the angel told us so."

The Messiah? I thought. *The one long ago promised by God? The one who would set His people free? This tiny little baby, the Messiah?*

"His name is Jesus," Uncle Aaron whispered. "Jesus, Saviour."

I pondered this boy's name quietly in my heart and then glanced at his mother. She had laid down to rest. Was her baby boy the Messiah? Did she know?

That feeling of peace only intensified as I pondered these questions.

Oh how I wished my mother had come along with us. She needed to know this peace in her heart. She was a prisoner to her anger over losing my father. She so often lashed out at people, especially God. She needed to be set free.

When I got home, I tried to tell her about all that I had seen and experienced. I told her that I had seen Messiah and felt the most amazing peace come over my heart as I looked at this very special baby,

Mother would hear none of it. "There's no Messiah. Never was, never will be."

With that, she just went back to bed.

I remember that night like it was yesterday, not thirty years ago. I did, in fact, go on and become a shepherd. And mother became a bitter old woman.

One day, I travelled to Jerusalem for Passover and Mother came along with me to visit her sister. The procession went right by her sister's place. It wasn't a planned procession, not part of the Passover celebrations.

First we saw an angry mob shouting and carrying on. Then came the Roman soldiers—and, in the middle of them, a man carrying a cross. This man had been beaten and whipped. He was hardly recognizable, but there was something about him.

My heart jumped when I saw this man. I couldn't put my finger on it, but he ignited a very strange feeling in my heart.

Then I overheard the crowd shouting: "Crucify this traitor Jesus!"

Can it be? I wondered. *Can this be that tiny baby in the manger? The Messiah?*

After that night in the stable, I hadn't seen him again. I had heard lately that a man was teaching and healing, and some thought he might be the Messiah, but I had been too busy with work to follow up on these comments.

"See, I told you that your Jesus wasn't Messiah," Mother said, coming up behind me to watch the procession. "Just another failure."

At that very moment, Jesus looked directly at us and I felt that same peace come into my heart. Just like before, all the noise was silenced and it was just Jesus and me. It felt like time stood still.

Mother had her mouth open to utter some harsh words, but nothing came out. She just stared back at the man she had just cursed. Her eyes became moist and tears marked little trails down her cheeks.

When words finally came, the procession had long since passed. The words were no longer filled with anger and bitterness but love.

"Shepherd," she stammered. "He's a shepherd. He wore a shepherd's cloak. The Messiah… the good shepherd." Her eyes became very distant. "We are His people, the sheep of His pasture."

She was no longer in Jerusalem at Passover but somewhere else. She was a little girl sitting at the dinner table and her father was reading the Hebrew scriptures.

"We all, like sheep, have gone astray," she said. "Each one of us has turned to his own way, and the Lord has laid on Him the iniquity of us all."[22]

More silence, more tears, more remembering.

"Oh, Simon, I've wasted so much of life being angry at God for taking your father while saving a few wretched sheep. But now God's own Son, the Messiah, the good shepherd, is about to lay down His life for wretched sheep like me. Could God ever forgive me?"

"Yes, Mother. Yes, He does."

---

[22] Isaiah 53:6, NIV.

Untangled[23]

"**M**ommy, Mommy, come quick! Daddy is hanging upside down outside our living room window." Little Matthew sounded amused, but there was also a tinge of panic in his voice.

Audrey rushed into the living room. Sure enough, there was her beloved Mort hanging head down, feet up, his inverted face staring through the picture window at his wife.

A smile crept onto Audrey's lips—that is, until the danger of the situation registered in her mind. Fortunately, the safety harness had done its job and Mort hadn't done a faceplant into the frozen garden.

"Are you going to stare or help me?"

Mort's plea penetrated the glass and spurred Audrey into action. Out the door she raced.

"Get the stepladder out of the garage and put it under me."

Before he could say "a partridge in a pear tree," she had firmly planted the stepladder onto the frozen soil. Mort than began the laborious task of turning himself right-side-up so he could sit on top of the ladder and get out of the harness. Next he had to untangle what seemed like hundreds of feet of the bright twinkling Christmas lights wrapped around his legs. These luminescence beacons of Christmas not only were the cause of Mort's ungainly exit from the roof, but now their glow seemed to mock him, even claim victory over him.

---

[23] This story contains adult content.

When Mort had finally righted himself, he surveyed the damage. Rudolph had taken a header into the snow, his red nose extinguished. Santa had abandoned the chimney and was precariously perched in the gutter. Christmas would be different at the Carberry house this year, that was for sure.

The Monday morning after Mort's graceless fall, an even more serious fall from grace awaited him at the office. As he put his briefcase on his desk, he noticed a note from the manager of his department. He wanted to see Mort as soon as he got in.

The request was quite common, so Mort wasn't alarmed.

He walked the length of the hall on the fourteenth floor and knocked on the manager's door. Pleasantries were exchanged, including a chuckle at Mort's misfortune with the Christmas decorations.

"Is that really you hanging upside-down?" The manager asked. He held out his phone, showing a picture of Mort's mishap. It was an angle Mort hadn't seen yet.

"Yes, that's really me."

"Any injuries, other than to your pride?"

"No."

"Good, glad to hear it. Listen, the reason I asked you to come by this morning…" The manager assumed a more serious tone. "…is that we— and by we, I refer to the corporation—has a favour to ask of you. You're one of our brightest and best accountants. Your work is always spot-on. We can rely on you, always. Anyway, we're considering a takeover of a big competitor. Now, in order to facilitate the acquisition we need to be sure everyone over there is impressed by our operations. This is where you come in. We'd like you to make some minor… well, how shall I say this? Some minor adjustments to a couple of our financial statements. This will make us look to be in an even stronger position than we are. It'll help the whole deal to work."

Mort hadn't expected to hear this. While he wasn't very religious, he did have a very high standard of morality. He had never knowingly misrepresented any figures in any of his previous work. Nor had he ever been asked to do such a thing. He knew such things took place in the business world, but never here.

"Are you asking me not to be totally honest with a financial statement?" Mort asked.

"Well, not really. I'm sure there's a way you can make numbers work and be able to justify them. Besides, no one will ever know. This information will stay strictly between us and the other company. The regulators will never see these statements."

The manager sounded quite reassuring, but it didn't quiet Mort's conscience.

"I don't know, sir." His voice was shaky. "I've never done anything like this before. It really goes against my morality."

"Well, your morality wasn't on display last summer when you drove Jessica home after that late night business meeting."

Mort's heart sank. Jessica was an administrative assistant, and last July they'd attended a corporate meeting that had gone all day and well into the evening. When it was over, Jessica had asked Mort for a drive home. Her car was in the garage for repairs and she hadn't been comfortable taking public transit late at night.

Mort had hesitated in offering to drive Jessica home, since she had been flirting with him. He had rejected her advances, but a part of him had still been flattered. Even though he knew this was wrong, he found her attractive. He'd caught his mind wandering into forbidden places.

He shouldn't have given her the ride. But she *had* lived on his way home, and she had needed help…

When he'd pulled up to the entrance to her condo building, she hadn't automatically moved to open the door.

"Mort, why don't you come up to my place and have a drink?" she'd asked. "Just to unwind. It's been a very long, tiring day. Just stay ten minutes. Then you can be on your way."

This was more than flirting and Mort knew it. He knew what he had to say… but he didn't. What would one drink matter?

"Sure, I'll come up. But just for ten minutes."

Mort had parked the car and the two of them made their way up to Jessica's place. It was only a drink, and twenty minutes later Mort was on his way home.

"We only had a drink," he told his manager. "Just two friends unwinding after a busy day. Nothing happened."

"That's not what Jessica remembers. She has a much more... how shall I put it? An interesting version of the night's events." The manager was dead serious. "And if you don't go along with our little request, Jessica is prepared to make her version of the story public."

A sick feeling came over Mort. He would never ever consider cheating on his wife. Giving in to a little flirtation even once had caught him in a web of his own making.

"And by the way, if you call our bluff and stick by your story, you can clear out your desk and look for another job." The manager was playing hardball. "Your wife will also be told the whole story. You have twenty-four hours to decide."

Mort got no work done that day. He just sat at his desk and stewed. He was trapped, entangled in a real mess. If he gave in, he would be compromising his own integrity, and even opening himself up to an investigation. Possibly even criminal charges. But if he stood by his principles, he would have to explain what had happened to his wife.

There seemed to be no way out.

How could his life have gone from so good to so bad so fast? The ropes holding him prisoner were getting tighter. When he'd taken that header off the roof, he'd had his wife to help him. Who could he call now?

O what a tangled web we weave...

Mort didn't know where those words came from, but they sure described his life.

"God help me," he said, so loud that it startled him. God wasn't a part of his life, not at all. The Bible was no more than a fairy tale, God a fictional character. As for prayer? Well, it was nothing more than wishful thinking, speaking words into the emptiness of space.

But hadn't he just prayed?

As Mort contemplated this last question, he felt a presence in the room with him. He turned to see man sitting nearby in his visitor's chair. A man he had never seen before.

"Who are you?" Mort asked.

"You just asked for help. The Almighty heard your request and sent me to help." The visitor spoke in a quiet but firm voice. "What kind of a mess have you gotten yourself into? I specialize in messes." He hesitated a moment. "Hey, aren't you the guy who did the faceplant off his roof the other day? You were quite a hit in the lounge where we await our assignments. But I'm guessing your predicament has more to it than that misstep."

"A whole lot more," Mort remarked. "Who are you? Why should I trust you with my problems? You could be on the corporation's payroll, looking to make my life more difficult."

"Believe me, I'm not on any corporation's payroll. I told you. The Almighty sent me here to help."

"Almighty? Do you mean God?"

"That's the only Almighty there is. So what problem am I here to solve?"

"You know the fall I took off the roof? Well, this predicament is like a fall off a much greater stage."

For some reason, Mort trusted this guy. He was coming around to believing that the visitor was truly an emissary from heaven. Perhaps Mort was just so desperate for help that he would accept anything that came along, even a fantasy as off the wall as this.

Mort explained the whole sordid mess in all its grimy details. The visitor took in every word this broken man spoke. When Mort had finished emptying his heart, silence filled the office for what seemed like an eternity.

Finally, the visitor broke the quiet. "I take it you aren't a follower of the Almighty."

"That's right."

"But you prayed and asked the Almighty for help."

Mort wasn't going to hide the truth. "I guess I did. I ran out of options. I was desperate."

"That's good. That's good, Mort. You've begun the journey of setting all matters right." The visitor's words brought a strange sense of peace to Mort's heart. "Now, what I'm going to suggest is going to sound crazy. It'll go against all common sense and reason, but that's how it often is with the Almighty. His ways are not our ways. I'll just give it to you straight-up: you have to quit your job and to tell your wife the truth."

The visitor's words were crystal clear in Mort's ears. His response was just as clear. "That's not exactly what I wanted to hear."

"Do you have a better idea?"

"Well, no, but I was hoping the Almighty's help would be more… well, helpful. And less disruptive to my life. How will I end up further ahead if I'm unemployed and facing a separation from my wife, or worse? Her heart will break when I tell her about Jessica, even if nothing physical happened."

"Never underestimate the power of the Almighty to untangle the worst messes we create for ourselves." The visitor kept up a very hopeful and positive tone. "Mind you, it won't be easy, but remember that the Master can straighten out even the most crooked pathways. To be free of the entanglements we weave, we have to be willing to disengage from the world's ways, and sometimes even common sense, to trust the Almighty and His ways. Believe me, when we do that everything gets better. Better than we could ever imagine, even if we don't see it."

"I still don't know. It all sounds pretty risky."

"I'll tell you what. I'll leave you for twenty-four hours. That's when your manager wants an answer, right? I'll be back. If you decide to follow the way the Almighty has mapped out for you, I'll help you through it all."

A moment later, Mort was left alone in his office with nothing but his own very conflicted thoughts and the soft sound of Christmas music. That music usually calmed his heart and gladdened his heart. He liked the songs, even though he paid little attention to the lyrics. It was all part of the atmosphere of Christmas, and Mort surrounded himself with it every year.

While trying to figure out what to do, one of the religious carols came on. For some reason it caught his attention. He was no longer hearing just a favourite tune; the words seemed to jump out in front of him in bold letters.

O little town of Bethlehem,
How still we see thee lie!
Above thy deep and dreamless sleep
The silent stars go by.
Yet in thy dark streets shineth
The everlasting light;
The hopes and fears of all the years
Are met in thee tonight.[24]

His hopes and fears were on a collision course. Just twenty-four hours ago, he had been on a high. Christmas was just around the corner and despite the incident on his roof everything had been good. He had so much to look forward to.

Now life had tripped him up. His hopes had become his darkest fears. Christmas was certainly ruined, there was no doubt about that. No way would this turn out to be the most wonderful time of year... and maybe it never would again.

The words of the carol came back into Mort's mind and heart like they were right in front of him on a whiteboard: *"Yet in thy dark streets shineth the everlasting light..."* Was there a light that could remove the darkness that had filled his heart?

Mort knew that Christmas supposedly marked the birth of Jesus, though he had never celebrated that aspect of the season. Was it possible that Jesus was this everlasting light? Had He really brought light to a dark world, a world all tangled up in a way of life that only led to more darkness, a world trapped in a web of brokenness and sin? Had Jesus come to untangle that mess and set it free from the untenable entrapment people found themselves in?

He had never gone down this path before. It was like an inner voice was teaching, guiding, and even calming his anxieties in a strange way.

Mort looked at his watch and realized he should have been home half an hour ago. He grabbed his briefcase and headed out to the elevator.

---

[24] Phillips Brooks, "O Little Town of Bethlehem," 1868.

Twenty minutes later, he walked through the side door of his house. Audrey greeted him in the kitchen with a kiss and asked where the fish and chips were. Only then did Mort remember that he had promised to pick up the traditional English meal for dinner.

"I'm sorry, honey." Mort was truly apologetic, even more than usual. "I'll go right now and be back in fifteen."

"No, it's okay. There's a lasagna in the freezer. That'll do for tonight."

Audrey didn't seem upset over Mort's absentmindedness. This wasn't the first time such an incident had occurred.

After dinner, Audrey searched out Mort and found him in the TV room.

"You're quiet tonight," she said. "You hardly spoke during dinner and then you just slipped away without saying a word. And here you are, without even turning on the TV…"

Mort turned on the screen. Perhaps it would serve as a good diversion.

"I'm sorry for giving you the quiet treatment at dinner," he murmured. "It was a tough day at work. I guess I just need some time to decompress."

Audrey took the hint. "Well, I'll leave you to your thoughts. I have some chores that need attention."

With that, his wife stepped out of the room and Mort was left alone with his very torturous thoughts.

That's when the inner voice returned and began speaking to his heart. It took him back to the past Saturday morning, when he'd hung upside-down from the roof. All he'd been able to think of was what had led to his fall? He had spent his entire life obsessed by the lights and tinsel of Christmas, and now they seemed to have been the cause of a near tragic accident.

"But the fall was really just the culmination of a more tragic fall," the inner voice declared. "You've fallen into a life that leaves Jesus out in the cold. This holy time of year has been turned into a secular celebration of self and humanism. This kind of Christmas makes you feel good for a short time, but once January comes along the old feelings come roaring back, sometimes in more intense ways. The world's Christmas only brings temporary relief, but the original purpose of Christmas—

the coming of Jesus to untangle the world of all that's broken—has been pushed aside in favour of a shallow celebration that does nothing to bring hope. In fact, it leaves you feeling more like a prisoner, entangled in a way of life that doesn't satisfy."

The voice spoke clearly and brought conviction to Mort's heart. He was a good person, even a very good person. He was a man of integrity, yet he had to admit that he had erred in an appalling manner where Jessica was concerned. Being good wasn't good enough.

If Mort wanted to be set free from this web of hurt and pain, he would have to acknowledge his brokenness, and this included being totally honest with Audrey. It would also mean losing his job. He would no longer let the worldly trappings of Christmas keep him from the true meaning of the season.

He once again recalled the words of that hymn:

O holy child of Bethlehem,
Descend to us, we pray;
Cast out our sin and enter in;
Be born is us today.[25]

He prayed those words. Even before he was done, he felt a huge burden lift from his heart. It felt as though the shackles that bound him to the world were broken open, making him feel free for the very first time in his life. He knew he would have to travel some pretty rough terrain in the next few days, even months, and he could only pray that his wife forgave him and he could find another job...

"Mommy!" their son shouted, sounding excited. "Mommy, come quick! Daddy has the manger scene all set up in the front yard."

While Mort waited for Matt and Audrey to join him, he was visited once more by the voice of the Almighty who had been guiding him for the past year.

A voice of one calling: "In the wilderness prepare the way for
the Lord; make straight in the desert a highway for our

---

[25] Ibid.

God. Every valley shall be raised up, every mountain and hill made low; the rough ground shall become level, the rugged places a plain." (Isaiah 40:3–4)

The Birthday Party

I t was a rather peculiar invitation. I'd never received one like it. And normally I wouldn't have accepted such an invitation, but it was that festive time of year.

"Samantha. Am I right?"

I recognized the speaker as another student. Larry, I believe was his name. He was in a couple of my classes. We had chatted briefly on a couple of occasions.

"Yes. That's me."

"Listen, Samantha, how would you like to go to a birthday party?" Larry asked. "I know you mentioned a while back that you would be staying here for the holidays. The party is on the twenty-fourth, in the evening. It will be a really great time. A lot of other students and even a few faculty will be there."

It would be nice to have something to do, especially that night. It was the eve of one of the happiest days of the year, or so people said.

So I answered yes, even if it was the birthday party of someone I didn't know. In fact. someone I had never even met.

The next instruction from Larry, however had me second-guessing the invitation. Everyone was to bring a gift, a gift that would be suitable for either a male or for a female.

"Seriously?" I asked. "Can't you even tell me if this mystery person whose birthday we're celebrating is a man or woman?"

"Doesn't matter," Larry replied.

"Really?"

"Really!"

I was told to arrive any time after 7:00 p.m. on Friday evening. The dress was semi-casual, and I could bring a friend if I wished.

"This is going to be a pretty popular party," Larry said. "Probably the best attended one of the whole year. Once people hear you're going, they'll want to come too."

I'm not the kind of person to be spontaneous, but this time I felt a tug at my heart I couldn't refuse. I wasn't sure if it was mere curiosity to see how this rather bizarre party came off or a deeper attraction.

I awoke on Friday morning with two classes to attend. The last two of the semester. Then it would be two weeks off before the start of a new year and new semester.

But I wasn't thinking of either the classes or the time off. I was consumed with impatience to get to this party, for whatever reason I didn't know. And I felt uneasiness about it all.

I had gone out the night before and purchased a gift card for a local restaurant, and I'd dropped it into a nicer than usual birthday card. It cost me nearly nine dollars with tax. I never paid nine dollars for a greeting card! Not even for my best friends. But I did this time, for someone I didn't even know.

All day, the hands on the clock moved in slow motion. All I wanted was to get home, have a shower, and get to the party.

I got off the bus at the stop closest to the address I had been given. It was cold with a fresh covering of snow from that afternoon. The streetlights cast an eerie glow on the new fallen snow. I shivered, and not just because it was cold. Something odd was in the works; I could feel it.

I thought of turning around and going back to the apartment. After all, I could use the gift card for someone else. But my heart overruled my head and I walked on until I stood outside 1225 Noel Avenue.

It was a very old stone building. Before going in, I took a minute to evaluate the situation. Should I or shouldn't I?

I should.

I climbed the wide stairs that led to the beautiful double oak doors. I pulled and they opened effortlessly.

As I entered the brightly lit cloakroom, a formally dressed gentleman offered to take my coat. He also showed me the way to the party.

"Through those doors," he pointed. Before me stood two more doors, dark wood inlaid with brass. "The best party on earth."

I turned and moved toward the doors that led to apparent utopia. Standing by the entrance were a man and a woman, each dressed in red and green elf costumes, hats and all. The female elf handed me a card.

WELCOME TO THE PARTY
We are so very pleased you have joined us
for this festive occasion.
HAPPY HOLIDAYS!

I found myself in a large hall. The atmosphere was the exact opposite of the cold and dreary aura that had covered the earth outside like a heavy, cumbersome blanket. The hall was illuminated by lights of all sorts— coloured lights, strings of lights, red and green and blue and yellow lights, all hanging from the ceiling and draped around the windows. There was music, happy and jolly, nothing heavy or burdensome. The room was filled to capacity with partygoers, all laughing and eating and dancing. I only recognized a few from school. Most were strangers.

This hall looked like it had been a built for a large assembly of one kind or another. The deejay was set up on a platform at the far end of the hall.

But what really caught my eye were the windows. Tall, elegant windows with stained-glass, each one featuring people I didn't recognize. One in particular caught my attention; it depicted a handsome man cradling a sheep in His arms. His face spoke of peace, love, and compassion.

"Come on in," said the person who had invited me in. "Make yourself at home. There's a gift tree up front. Please place your gift either under the tree or among the branches. You may retrieve your gift when it's time to exchange gifts."

"Exchanging gifts? I thought we're celebrating a birthday. Won't we be giving our gifts to the guest of honour?"

"Yeah! Yeah! Whatever. It will all work out, you'll see."

And with that, the man disappeared, lost in the crowd of partygoers.

I looked around and, sure enough, there was a huge tree decorated with lights and sparkly things. It stood on an elevated platform that seemed to have been situated in a place of honour. People were taking pictures in front of it.

"Isn't it the most beautiful tree?" someone asked when they caught me staring. "I just love it. It's so divine. I wouldn't miss coming here for anything, if only to see the tree."

I stepped forward to leave my gift by the tree, but at the last moment I decided to hang on to my card and gift. I didn't know why I made that decision. Everyone here seemed okay. I just felt like I needed to keep the gift with me.

By now, the party was in full swing. Music was playing, music that lifted my spirits to a level of peace I hadn't experienced before. Every table was piled high with food and beverages.

I spotted a classmate, someone I sat next to in calculus. I didn't even know his name, but I needed answers. What better place to start?

"Hey!" I called.

"Hey, yourself," he answered. "You look familiar… oh yeah, next to me in calculus. Isn't this a great party?"

"Yeah, great." I tried to sound enthusiastic. "Listen, do you know whose birthday we're celebrating? Perhaps you could point them out to me."

"I'm actually not sure of their name. I don't know much. But every year—this is my third year here—we have this party for them. Come to think of it, I don't even recall meeting them. It's just the best party of the year. I wouldn't miss it. Everyone is so positive and in such a good mood. Even some who are normally a bit grumpy put on their smiley faces for this. It seems to bring out the best in people. The feeling lasts well into next week! But then it's back to the normal grind, burdens and all."

I moved on, more perplexed than ever. I did have to admit the party was pretty cool. Everyone was friendly and I heard lots of laughter and good wishes.

A total stranger approached. "Hey friend! Is this beautiful or what? This is my ninth year. I graduated five years ago but still come back to the party. It's a five-hour drive but totally worth it."

"You drive five hours just to come to a birthday party of someone you don't know? You don't know the person whose birthday it is, do you?"

"No, never met them. Don't even know their name."

"Then why come?"

"It's the atmosphere, the attitude," he said. "It's the one time of year when everyone is so kind. It's like all the uglies are checked at the door. There are no mean words, no selfishness. We're in a great big love bubble."

I frowned. "Do you know how many years this party has been held?"

"No, not at all. Though I did hear once that we've passed the one hundred year anniversary. But I don't think it was always like this. I understand things were different years ago."

This really puzzled me. A birthday party that was a hundred years old? What was that all about? Whoever's birthday we were celebrating would have long died.

I made several more inquiries about whose birthday we were celebrating, but no one knew. I just kept hearing that this was the best party of the whole year. And I had to agree.

All this sleuthing had made me hungry. I'd been at the party for more than an hour and hadn't sat down once.

I looked around for a table with an empty seat. There, near the back of the room was just such a table, with only one person sitting at it. There were three plates, however, piled high with sandwiches. A welcome sight for a very empty stomach.

A minute later, there were two people sitting at this table.

I reached out my hand. "Hi, I'm…"

The other guest completed my sentence. "Samantha Engle, second-year student studying applied science. It's your first time at the party."

How did he know my name? Startled, I got up to leave. This guy knew too much.

"Don't go," he said. "Really, I would love you to stay."

"But… but…"

"I know what it must sound like, but I'm really an okay person."

I stopped myself, half-standing, and studied the stranger. I mean, he looked okay, even gentle. There even seemed to be a sadness about him which made him stand out from everyone else. The others all laughed and joked and carried on having a great time, but not this chap.

I began to feel sorry for him, but just for a minute. I would stay, for his sake, but I didn't want to let my guard down.

As I sat back down, a smile broke through his sadness.

"Are you from around here?" I asked.

"I'm from here and there. I travel and have seen a lot of the world. No, make that all of the world. I'm from away and I'm from close."

"Do you know the guest of honour? You know, the one whose birthday we're celebrating?"

"Yes, I know them very well." He paused, as if he was going to say more but then decided against it.

"Well, do you care to share with me who this mystery person is?"

"Oh, you'll find out soon enough."

More mystery. This guy seemed to talk in riddles. I had more questions than answers.

Our conversation was interrupted when the music stopped, as did all the chatter and laughter. The one who had first invited me into the room was standing at the microphone.

"I want to thank all of you for coming tonight. It's my favourite time of year. There's so much goodwill and love in the air. And the music, isn't it wonderful?" He paused for a moment. "Now it's time to exchange gifts. Those of you who've been here before know the routine. For all of you first-timers, here's what we do. Find someone you don't know and invite them to be your gift partner. If they agree, and they always do, then the two of you will exchange gifts."

People started to move around, but the person at the microphone asked them to stay put for one more minute.

"Before we move off, I want us to observe a moment's silence in honour of the one whose birthday we're celebrating. While we don't know their name, I do think we should honour the one who has made all this possible."

As these last few words were spoken, I looked at my tablemate and was sure I could see a tear in his eyes. When he saw me looking, he glanced away.

After a minute or two of silence, people began moving around the room, each one looking for someone with whom to exchange gifts.

Why move? I thought. *Why not give my gift to this person sitting right here with me, even if he was a little different?*

"New friend, I'd like to give my gift to you," I said.

He turned and looked right at me. When his eyes met mine, they were filled with more love and compassion than I had ever seen or felt before. A smile crossed his lips and the sadness lifted.

"I've been coming here since the very first party," he said. "And no one has ever taken the time to sit with me. And when it comes time to exchange gifts, no one has even approached me. Not once. Everyone loves the party. It will go on for several more hours. And I'll slip out in a while. I won't hang around. I won't be missed."

With these last words, my heart broke into a thousand pieces. But this stranger wasn't really a stranger, was he? He was becoming a friend.

"You're the guest of honour, aren't you?" I suddenly realized. "It's your birthday. But all these others, they don't know you. They don't even recognize you." I looked to the stained-glass window. "That's you in the picture window. You are the one holding a sheep."

He smiled an even wider smile than his first and the peace in my heart morphed into love, a love beyond explanation. I felt loved like I had never been loved before. Life had been tough. My father left my mother when I was six months old. My mother had tried but just couldn't cope, so before my first birthday I had been placed in a foster home. And there I stayed, a ward of the province, until I was sixteen. Some foster parents were better than others, but from none did I really feel love. I felt pity and even sympathy, but not real love.

At sixteen, I had vowed to myself that I would make something of my life, so I finished high school with honours and went on to study science with the hope of being a doctor someday.

But now the love I felt from this man, this pure, unconditional love, pierced my heart and lifted me up to a place I had never been before.

I held out my card and he took it. I thought my heart would bust. I'd never felt anything like this before. It was like being offered the most priceless gift in the world.

As he took the card from me, I noticed the nail prints in the palms of his hands.

His gift to me.

He was in the world, and though the world was made through him, the world did not recognize him. He came to that which was his own, but his own did not receive him. Yet to all who did receive him, to those who believed in his name, he gave the right to become children of God—children born not of natural descent, nor of human decision or a husband's will, but born of God. (John 1:10–13)

The Return of the Shepherd

Roger turned to enter the driveway and there it was, just as it had been in the morning when he'd left for work: a driveway full of snow. It had been a very long day with more problems than solutions, and now it was 11:00 p.m. The problem in front of him? Well, let's say the lid came off the pressure cooker.

After getting the SUV off the street, Roger marched into the house and down to Jason's room. No knock. He just barged in to find his son planted in front of the game console.

"You know what I found just now?" Roger's voice would have made thunder cower. "I found a driveway full of snow. A driveway I specifically asked you to shovel before I left this morning. That's the least you could have done. What did you do all day? Sit around and play games with all your online buddies? What, they don't have to shovel snow, so you figure neither do you? I know you're out of work, but you're not out of family. If you're going to live here, you have to pull your own weight. I don't see much evidence that you're at all invested in this family. In name only, I guess." Roger was just warming up. "You only do what suits you and blow us off the rest of the time. Somehow you think you can stay a member of this family and enjoy all the perks without really being committed to it. You eat our food, use our electricity, and we get nothing back except excuses. You're a user loser."

Before he finished uttering those last words, he knew he had crossed the line.

Jason looked at his enraged father, stood up, and walked out of the room. Roger stood silently, not able to move a muscle. He jumped when he heard the side door slam shut.

"Roger, what have you done? Where's Jason?" It was Allison, Roger's wife, calling downstairs.

"Don't get on my case, Allison. It's not my fault he's gone. He knows the rules. If he'd follow them, everything would be just fine."

Roger climbed the stairs, walked over to the door, and began putting his shoes on.

"I'm going out to get some fresh air."

"At this time of night?" his wife asked. It's nearly midnight."

"Goodbye."

With that, the door slammed for the second time in less than ten minutes.

Roger got into his SUV and began driving to no place in particular. Soon he found himself in an older part of town, a part he hadn't visited in a very long time. He couldn't remember the last time he'd been there, but for some reason he had felt drawn to drive that way.

While waiting for a light to turn green, he noticed an all-night coffee shop two doors up from the corner. Its open sign flashed red.

He hadn't intended to stop. He really didn't want anything, but he found himself parking across the deserted street from this dispensary of caffeine.

Well, I'm here, thought Roger. *I may as well go in and have a coffee. Maybe it will clear my mind.*

As he pushed open the old wooden door, a bell rang to let whoever was working this graveyard shift know that they had a customer. No one appeared.

Roger spied a table near the back and made his way there.

"I thought I'd find you here," a voice called as though out of nowhere. "Boss told me to get down here real fast, so here I am. What's wrong this time?"

This time? Roger wondered to himself. *When was the last time?*

Then it hit him. He looked around and a cold chill travelled down his spine. It all came back to him. He *had* been here before.

He turned toward the sound of the voice. Walking toward him was a rough-looking character who was all too familiar.

"Remember me? I'm Shepherd," the man said. "We met here twenty-nine years ago, give or take a few months. Do you mind if I sit down, or do I do this standing up? My legs aren't as strong as before. All those nights out in the fields and the cool and damp air. Reckon I got a double case of rheumatoid arthritis—mine and yours. Ha! Shepherd's laugh quickly became a cough. "Night air's hard on the lungs too."

Roger motioned for Shepherd to sit down. He was in too much shock to speak. He tried to open his mouth, but nothing came out.

Shepherd gathered his robes up around him and sat down. "Boss called me out of retirement for this one, so it had better be good. I was having a great sleep back at Grasslands Acres. It's a retirement home for shepherds. Their slogan is 'We make ewe feel right at home.' Get it? Ewe... female sheep... and we're shepherds. Pretty clever. Ha!" He lapsed into another coughing spell. "Anyway, we're not here to talk about me. What's up, Roger?"

Before Roger could say a word, a young lad of maybe sixteen years appeared at the table with two cups of steaming hot coffee.

"One black for the shepherd, one double cream no sugar for the troubled-looking man," the boy said. "Just like last time."

Roger found his voice. "But you weren't even born last time we were here. How do you know what we had last time?"

"Boss told me."

As far as Roger could determine, there was no one else in the coffee shop, not even in the kitchen. He heard no voices, nothing. He could feel the hairs on the back of his neck stand up.

"That'll be four dollars and fifty-nine cents."

"I've got it this time." Shepherd reached deep into the folds of his robes and pulled out a five-dollar bill. "Here, keep the change."

"Sorry, sir, we don't take cash. Just debit, credit, or e-payment."

"But I remembered to change my money this time." Shepherd looked confused. "Just so I could pay."

Roger came to the rescue. "Here, I'll take care of this." He touched his phone to the portable pay machine, which emitted a single beep.

"Electronic?" Shepherd said it like it was a question.

Roger looked up after putting his phone back in his pocket. "You don't even want to know, my friend."

"So are you going to tell me what's up or do I have to guess?"

"Had a fight with my son and he walked out of the house." Roger spoke clearly but quietly.

"Last time it was your father who had a fight with you and kicked you out of the house."

Roger felt very uncomfortable. This was all very strange to him.

His thoughts took him back all those years. He remembered sitting at this very table. It had been Christmas Eve when this same shepherd appeared. For the very first time in his life, Roger had discovered what Christmas was really all about. It was about love, God's love for him personally. Shepherd had told him that God loved him so much that He'd been willing to give up His very own son and send Him to earth. Though his earthly father had ejected him, Roger had learned that night that he had a heavenly Father and a Saviour who had died on a cross for him. Shepherd had said he would throw in Easter at no extra cost. You really couldn't have Christmas without Easter.

After the shepherd had challenged him to give his heart to Jesus, Roger had done exactly that. God had taken care of him ever since. Roger had gone from being a homeless and harassed nineteen-year-old to being a beloved child of God.

He had searched for a church and joined one. That's where he had met His wife. They'd two children, Jason and Rachel.

As much as he had never wanted to be part of the corporate world, it had chased him until he gave in. Now he owned seven popular coffee shop franchises.

After he finished catching Shepherd up on how his life had gone, the man leaned forward. "Very interesting. So how's church going? How's your relationship with Jesus?"

Roger fell silent. Shepherd had such a kind face and his smile was gentle and caring. That only made things worse for Roger.

The silence grew. Shepherd didn't push; he just waited.

When Roger couldn't stand the silence any longer, he spoke. "I don't go to church much anymore. I kind of got away from it. I still believe. That hasn't changed. It's just that… well, you know, the kids have all their activities on Sunday and there really isn't any other time than Sunday to get the chores done around the house. And the guys on the men's ball team I play on make a good point. You can worship God anywhere. I didn't argue with them on that point."

The tone of Roger's voice seemed to suggest he was trying to convince himself of the legitimacy of all these excuses.

"So you're a silent Christian," Shepherd mused.

"A silent Christian?"

"A silent Christian. You believe in your heart that you're still a faithful follower of Jesus, or at least you tell yourself that, but by your words and actions you aren't there for Him. You enjoy all the perks without pulling your weight as a member of the God's family. Someone who didn't know you would never guess that you're part of God's family. As a matter of fact, they might think just the opposite. You're a silent Christian. You even had a hand in putting Jesus to death, all because of your silence."

These words stung Roger's heart. He knew he wasn't the best Christian around, but he didn't appreciate this analysis at all.

He shifted in his chair. Another long silence ensued.

Shepherd's raspy voice broke that silence. "Come."

Before Roger could react, the gingham tablecloth with the red and white squares disappeared, as did the smell of coffee brewing. It was replaced by the smell of a woodfire and the murmur of low voices.

Wherever he was, it was outside. It was nighttime and the sky was oppressively dark. It looked like a walled courtyard of some type. The cool breeze forced him to pull the collar of his jacket up around his neck.

Roger noticed the source of the burning wood. A small campfire was smouldering in the middle of the courtyard. Several soldiers sat warming themselves by the fire.

There was also another man sitting nearby. A very large man dressed not like a soldier, but a labourer. As the soldiers laughed at crude jokes, the civilian remained quiet, nervously taking in their tall tales. He glanced around furtively, as though hoping no one would recognize him.

One of the soldiers turned to him at last. "I know who you are. You were with Him in the garden when we arrested Him. You're one of His followers."

"I am not!" The man spoke so forcefully that his tone spooked Roger.

The soldier who had spoken now turned to his friends. "He denies knowing Him when even that girl at the gate confronted him about it…"

Just then, a servant appeared in the courtyard. He walked right up to the civilian.

"You *were* with Him," said the servant. "Sure you were. I saw you with Him in the garden."

"No!" the man thundered.

Everyone stopped what they were doing and looked right at him. A rooster crowed in the background.

Suddenly, the main let out a scream. The wail of an utterly broken man.

A cold chill ran through Roger's veins as the man looked up, his face lit by the firelight. The man looked exactly like Roger himself. It was Roger's face! And he had just denied Jesus.

Roger looked away as quickly as possible. He fixed his eyes on Shepherd, standing in the shadows.

That's not me, Roger wanted to shout. *I didn't deny Jesus.*

But he knew that it was him, and that Shepherd was right.

Shepherd gestured for Roger to come closer. Roger couldn't get away from the fire fast enough.

"Can we go back now?" It wasn't so much a question as an earnest plea.

"Not yet," said Shepherd. "There's one more thing I want you to see. But I have to warn you, it's not a pretty sight."

"What did I do this time?"

"It's not you, it's me." Shepherd paused. "And sort of you."

While trying to decipher this mystery, Roger found himself transported to a sunlit street filled with a riotous crowd. The building in front of him reminded him of city hall back home, although it differed in one major way; it had an open porch at the front.

And on that porch stood a Roman official of high standing. Next to him was a man, bloodied and beaten.

A sick feeling came over Roger. He wanted to throw up, for he knew this story only too well. Pilate was trying to give his verdict, a verdict that favoured the beaten man, Jesus, but the angry crowd was shouting: "Crucify Him! Crucify Him!"

Finally, Pilate threw His hands up in the air and the crowd quieted right down.

"I find no reason to give this man the death sentence, but go ahead, have your way." He turned to the soldiers on guard. He spoke through gritted teeth. "Crucify this man."

The crowd roared their approval.

Roger looked over the crowd and spotted Shepherd at the back, his face contorted with sorrow. His lips didn't move as he stood silently.

Say something, Roger wanted to shout. *You know who He is. You were there when He was born.*

But he dared not open his mouth. If he said anything, the crowd might turn on him.

Shame burned like a torch in Roger's heart, but still the words didn't come. He stood mute while Jesus was led away to be executed—and it was because of his own silence.

Because of Shepherd's silence.

Roger and Shepherd joined the procession out to the place of crucifixion. They walked side by side, saying nothing to each other all the way out.

Once at the execution site, however, they separated.

The crowd was huge, the people still hurling insults, taunting and pouring out scorn on this poor innocent prisoner. Even as He was raised up on His cross, the mocking increased.

Roger watched from a distance, listening and watching this whole ugly drama play out. As for Shepherd, he was totally distraught. Sorrow filled every pore on His face, but he too remained silent.

Suddenly the hot, humid air was replaced by a cool, fresh breeze. The loud crowd vanished, replaced by deafening silence.

We were back in the coffee shop. The gingham tablecloth had reappeared in front of Roger with two empty coffee cups on it.

Shepherd's usual smile and was gone. In its place was a sadness Roger had never seen in him before.

Roger didn't know what to say. The silence lasted for what seemed a lifetime.

"I'm no better than Peter," Shepherd said slowly. He was surprisingly quiet compared to his usual booming voice. "I didn't speak up. Not one voice offered support for Jesus. Not one voice called for Jesus not to be crucified. Not one voice tried to stop the insults, to counter the hate. I stood by and watched in silence. My Father in heaven gave me the privilege of being there when Jesus was born and I heard the angels sing their mighty Hallelujah chorus from the heavens. I saw the baby Messiah in the manger. Me. Yes, God gave me that awesome privilege. But when Jesus needed me most, I shut down on Him."

Shepherd looked down at the floor.

"He didn't shut down on us," Roger said, his voice equally quiet. "He spoke up loud and clear for us. Maybe not with His voice, but His actions spoke thousands of words. Words of love and grace and forgiveness."

Roger dragged the last few words out. It slowly dawned on him what he was saying.

Shepherd looked up. A slight smile had returned to his lips, the peace returned to his face.

"It's about love," Roger added. "Unconditional, sacrificial love. His love for us and our love for Him. And it's about speaking up for that love. It's about living out that love in our lives every day."

These words spilled out of Roger's mouth unrehearsed, like a river overflowing its banks onto dry, parched land.

Shepherd nodded. His smile grew larger.

The bells over the door of the coffee shop jingled and Shepherd glanced up. He gestured for the new customer to come and join he and Roger.

When Roger turned to see who had come into the shop, he saw that it was Jason. The young man spotted his father and stopped midstep.

Silence. As the long seconds passed, Jason took slow steps forward until he stood before the table where Roger sat.

"You know Shepherd?" Roger asked.

"We met earlier tonight." Jason sounded unsure of himself. "He helped me clear up some stuff. He showed me a new way to look at life."

Roger thought about this for a moment and then motioned for Jason to sit with them.

The young waiter approached the table again. He placed a plate of broken bread and a cup filled with wine on the red gingham tablecloth...

www.ingramcontent.com/pod-product-compliance
Lightning Source LLC
Chambersburg PA
CBHW061250170626
46809CB00007B/2927